Doughnuts and Deception

A
Peridale Cafe
MYSTERY

AGATHA FROST

Other books in the Peridale Café Series

A

Peridale Cafe
MYSTERY

Book Three

CHAPTER 1

J ulia reached under her bed, her fingers closing around the baseball bat. Her gran, Dot, had given it to her three weeks ago, insisting that it wasn't safe for a single woman to be living alone, especially with the recent murders. Julia hadn't taken her seriously, but had put it under her bed all the same, just in case. As she picked up the bat, she was glad for the gift.

With the wooden bat in hand, she tiptoed

towards her bedroom door. Holding her breath, she pressed her ear up against the cold oak, wanting to be sure she hadn't imagined the rustling that had woken her. The unmistakable zip of a backpack confirmed her suspicions.

She twisted the brass doorknob, wincing as the old cottage creaked around her. She didn't know what she was going to do when she came face-to-face with the mystery person digging in her kitchen, but she hoped the bat would scare them off before she had to find out if she had a good swing.

"I've called the police!" she cried out, the shake in her voice betraying her. "I'm armed!"

The rustling stopped, and then something smashed against the tiles in her kitchen. Acting fast, she reached out and slapped for the hallway light, her fingertips narrowly missing the switch in the dark. She stepped on something fluffy, which let out an ear-piercing yowl. Jumping back, her bare heel caught the edge of her hallway rug, sending her tumbling backwards, the bat flying free in the air. She opened her eyes as gravity sent the bat soaring back towards her face. Rolling out of the way just in time, she crashed into the small table displaying the dozen roses Barker had given her. The bat clattered against the floor as she darted forward, catching the vase before it succumbed to a similar fate.

"Julia?" Jessie cried, running out of the kitchen, fully dressed and clutching a backpack. "What are you doing?"

Jessie flicked on the light Julia had been reaching for before she stepped on Mowgli, who was now cowering by the front door, sending daggers in her direction. Squinting at the light, she looked down at the vase of roses she was holding in her lap.

"I thought you were a burglar," Julia mumbled feebly, glancing awkwardly to the bat.

Jessie took the vase from Julia and placed it back where it belonged. "You keep a baseball bat under your bed? You're more gangsta than I thought, cake lady."

Julia gratefully accepted Jessie's offer of a hand. Standing on both feet, she realised she had acted thoughtlessly in her sleepy state. Her gran's fear mongering had worked.

"Are you sleepwalking again?" Julia asked as she leaned over to pick up the bat.

Jessie looked down at her clothes and then up at Julia, arching a dark brow. She was wearing her Doc Martins, baggy jeans ripped at the knees, and a heavy hoodie. They were the clothes she had worn when Julia had caught her stealing from her café two months ago, before she had offered Jessie a job and the use of her guest bedroom.

"I had a dream," Jessie said, tossing the full backpack over her shoulder. "I'll explain it over a cup of tea."

Julia followed Jessie through to the kitchen, where all the drawers and cupboards were wide open. Julia's favourite cat-shaped mug was scattered across her kitchen floor in pieces, having fallen victim to Jessie's rummaging. Julia sat at her kitchen counter, scratching her head as she let out a yawn. The cat clock, with its swinging tail and darting eyes, told her it was only five in the morning.

"I had a dream," Jessie repeated, staring out into the dark garden as she filled the kettle. "I was homeless again. It felt so real."

"It was just a dream," Julia offered, as comfortingly as she could. "You don't ever have to worry about being homeless again. I won't let that happen."

Jessie smiled over her shoulder as she set the kettle back in its stand. She plucked two individually wrapped teabags from the box in the cupboard and ripped them open with her teeth before dropping them into two mugs. While the kettle boiled, she fished the dustpan and brush from under the sink and started to clean up the shattered cat mug.

"I'll replace it," Jessie said as she swept up the pieces. "I'm sorry. I panicked. I don't want you to think I was robbing you."

Julia cast an eye over to the bag, and then to her kitchen cupboards. It appeared that most of her food had made its way into the bulging backpack.

"It's just a mug," Julia said, shrugging and ignoring the small pang in her chest as she watched Jessie toss it into the bin. "I'll get over it."

Jessie smiled again, but her young face was solemn. Julia wondered how bad the dream had been.

"I was back on the streets," Jessie continued, pouring the boiling water into the two mugs. "Back at the old Fenton Industrial Park. That's where I was most of the time."

Julia had heard of Fenton Industrial Park more than once. It was a couple of miles from Peridale, on the outskirts of Cheltenham. *The Peridale Post* had covered the devastating fire that had caused all the businesses to flee the area. What it hadn't covered was that a small community of homeless people had moved in and made the area their own soon after, but she had heard that on the Peridale grapevine.

"I know of it," Julia said with a nod as Jessie set

a cup in front of her. "I can't imagine that being an easy way to live."

"It wasn't," Jessie said, sitting across from Julia, the dark circles under her eyes becoming obvious. "It was a horrible place to live, if I'm being honest, but it was home for six months. It felt more like six years. The winter seemed to go on forever, but we had each other, y'know? We were sort of a family. We watched each other's backs and protected each other. When I used to nick cakes from your café, I'd take whatever I could back and share them out."

"That was very thoughtful of you," Julia said, blowing the edge of her scalding hot tea. "You're a nice girl, Jessie."

"But I'm not, am I?" she cried, her voice suddenly shooting up. "Because I got this cushy new life and left them all there to get on with it."

"Is that what the bag is about?"

Jessie glanced to the bag and nodded.

"I woke up in a cold sweat," she said, staring into her cup as the teabag steeped, its golden goodness swirling in small circles. "I felt so guilty. I left to find some food two months ago and never went back, not even to explain."

"Were you going back there?"

"Only to give them food," Jessie said, looking

ahead at the empty cupboards. "I would have replaced it all before you woke up. I made a list."

Jessie reached into her pocket and pulled out a crumpled, messily written shopping list. Julia smiled, resting her hand on top of Jessie's.

"I don't care about the food," Julia said. "As long as you're safe, that's all I care about."

"I wouldn't trade this in for nothin'," Jessie looked around the small kitchen, as though she was taking in a grand castle. "But the others aren't so lucky, are they?"

Julia sipped her tea, the cogs in her brain churning at lightspeed. She had wanted to ask Jessie about her days of being homeless ever since first meeting her, but she hadn't wanted to appear nosy. Gossiping was the number one pastime in Peridale, and Julia hadn't wanted Jessie to think she was just another village snoop.

"I've got an idea," Julia said after taking another sip, the liquorice tickling the back of her throat. "Go back to sleep and we'll visit Fenton Industrial Park together when the sun has risen. We don't want to arrive when everyone is still asleep, do we?"

Chewing the inside of her cheek, Jessie looked at the bag again. She seemed to want to grab it and run straight for the door, but Julia trusted her to see the sense in what she was offering.

"I guess," Jessie said, shrugging and letting out a yawn. "You don't have to come."

"I want to."

Jessie took a sip of her tea, but as usual, she didn't finish it. She slid off the stool and hovered next to Julia, looking like she wanted to say something. Instead, she wrapped her arms around Julia's chest, squeezing tightly. Closing her eyes, she rested her hands on Jessie's arms, smiling to herself.

"Go on! Back to bed!" Julia ordered, tapping Jessie's arms. "I'll wake you in a couple of hours."

Jessie let go and headed back to her bedroom. Julia waited until she heard the creaking of Jessie's metal bed-frame before she stood up. As she unloaded Jessie's bag and returned the food to her kitchen cupboards, she tried to remember her mum's old recipe for doughnuts.

CHAPTER 2

L ooping around the roundabout for a second time, Julia glanced over to Jessie, who had trays of doughnuts stacked up on her knees. Fumbling with her hands on top of the plastic wrap securing the doughnuts in place, she cracked her knuckles again. She had been doing it since they had left the cottage.

"You don't have to be nervous," Julia said,

finally taking the turn after driving around a third time. "I'll be by your side the entire time."

Jessie didn't seem to have heard her. She stared ahead, continuing to crack her knuckles; the sound sending a shiver down Julia's spine.

From the moment Julia had woken Jessie soon after sunrise, she had sensed the girl's fear. It didn't surprise Julia. While she had been baking over one hundred doughnuts for the homeless residents of Fenton Industrial Park, Julia had wondered if returning there was the best thing for Jessie. Despite Jessie's protests that she wasn't leaving Julia, something deep within her squirmed uncomfortably.

"We're here," Julia said, the burnt husk of the industrial park coming into view.

Jessie snapped out of her trance state and stared ahead at the blackened warehouse buildings, which looked like they could fall to the ground at any moment. Fingers tightening around the steering wheel, Julia hated the thought of this being home to anybody, let alone a teenage girl.

They pulled up outside of the industrial park, and it had a huge 'FOR SALE' sign looming next to the entrance, which in turn had a 'SALE BY AUCTION' sticker plastered across its front, with an auction date only a couple of weeks away.

Doughnuts and Deception

Through the spiked, metal fences, Julia spotted the community Jessie had spoken about, and her heart skipped a beat.

"There's so many people," Julia whispered, the words escaping her mouth before she even had a chance to think about them.

"The country's hidden problem," Jessie said with wisdom beyond her sixteen years. "We – I mean – *they* live in places like this because it's easier for people to pretend we – I mean - *they* don't exist."

Julia wanted to tell her that wasn't true, but she bit her tongue before she let a lie slip out. She thought of her own perception of homeless people before she had met Jessie. There was nobody that she knew of in Peridale who was homeless. Until she caught Jessie breaking into her café, it always felt like an issue that happened in other parts of the country. Yet here she was, staring through the gaps in the metal fence at dozens of people, less than an hour's drive from her front door. During her time living in London, there were homeless men and women on every corner asking for spare change. She would often dig a pound coin out of her purse for the most desperate looking of them, but there were so many it was impossible to help all of them. It was a problem most city folk were overly desensitised to. They blended into the pavement, huddled in doorways under rags while the rest of the world got on with their comfortable lives. Jessie was right, they were hidden, but Julia wondered if that was by choice, or because the rest of the country had stopped noticing them.

After what felt like an age of staring, Julia twisted her keys in the ignition and drove through the broken down gates. Men and women were huddled around make-shift fires in burnt out barrels, others hiding from the early morning sunlight under blankets. Heads turned towards Julia's vintage aqua blue Ford Anglia, but most didn't bat an eyelid. She drove into an empty corner and jammed the handbrake in place. She glanced at the backseat at the stacks of doughnuts. When she had left her cottage, she had been sure she had baked enough to have leftovers to sell in the café on Monday morning, but that hope quickly vanished.

Julia jumped out of her car and opened her boot. She dragged out her old folding wallpaper-pasting table and kicked it open, fastening the small hinges into place. After throwing a pale pink and blue picnic blanket over its tarnished surface, she heaved a giant Victorian silver coffee maker out of her car and placed it carefully on the rickety table.

Doughnuts and Deception

Taking the lid off the huge vat, she inhaled the still hot, rich coffee. She had been looking for an excuse to use the contraption since picking it up at a carboot sale over a year ago.

Jessie finally got out of the car and placed the doughnuts on the table, while Julia arranged the small cardboard cups, bag of sugar cubes taken from her café, and a box of coffee whitener.

"Coffee and doughnuts!" Julia announced, cupping her hands around her mouth. "Free coffee and doughnuts to all who want them!"

All heads turned to Julia this time and a line quickly formed in front of the table. Jessie handed out the doughnuts while Julia poured coffee from a tap jutting out of an ornate lion's mouth embedded in the coffee maker. People accepted their free sweet treat and hot drink while gratefully muttering their thanks.

"Jessie?" an old worn voice called from the crowd of faces. "I thought that was you!"

A slender, elderly man hobbled forward with the assistance of a wooden walking stick that had been patched up with duct tape in more than one spot. His grey hair was long and scraggly, cheekbones high and sharp, sunken eyes, and a heavy brow casting dark shadows over his face. He looked like he had the ability to look menacing without much effort, but his ear-to-ear smile was so warm, Julia wasn't sure the man possessed a mean-spirited bone in his body.

"Tommy!" Jessie cried, matching his smile.

The old man broke through the line and embraced Jessie with one arm as he steadied himself with his stick. Jessie on the other hand gripped the man around the waist and buried her face into his mucky clothes. It brought a smile to Julia's face as she continued to serve coffee and doughnuts.

When Jessie finally let go of the man, they moved around to the front of Julia's car to talk. Julia served the rest of the people in the line as quickly as she could. When she ran out of coffee and only the crumbs of the doughnuts were left, she wiped her fingers down the front of her pale peach 1940s style dress before joining Jessie and the old man she had called Tommy.

"I've been hearing all about you," Tommy said, holding a hand out to Julia. "If I had a hat, I would take it off to you ma'dear."

Julia accepted the man's weathered hand. The strength of his grip surprised her.

"I just did what any other decent person would do," Julia said, smiling at Jessie.

Doughnuts and Deception

"I don't think every person who calls themselves decent would take in a girl from the streets," Tommy assured her. "You really are a marvellous woman. And an incredible baker too. Jessie would bring your cakes back here when she – y'know – *borrowed* them."

"I saved you one." Julia pulled a doughnut wrapped in a paper napkin out of her dress pocket. "There's no coffee left I'm afraid."

"I never did like the stuff much," Tommy said, tipping his head to Julia as he accepted and pocketed the doughnut in one of his filthy overcoat pockets. "Not good for the heart at my age."

Julia tried to place the man's age, but she couldn't quite figure it out. His almost skeletal frame and the layer of grime covering his deeply wrinkled skin aged him, but there was a twinkle in his eyes and a youth to his smile that made her think he was younger than he appeared. She placed him in his mid-to-late sixties. Something told her he wasn't much older than her own father.

Tommy took them across the car park to a small doorway in one of the burnt out warehouses. Black smudges lined the metal door, and it didn't take much of Julia's imagination to visualise the flames licking the air as they tried to escape the grand metallic structure.

With his fumbling fingers, Tommy pulled two upturned plastic crates together and tossed a well-worn red blanket over them. He motioned for Jessie and Julia to take a seat as he opted to sit cross-legged on a folded up sleeping bag in the doorway. Julia realised she was in the man's home.

"Tommy's in charge 'round here," Jessie said. "What he says goes."

"I don't know about that, little one," Tommy laughed as he pulled the squashed up doughnut from his pocket. "People here come and go and do what they please."

Julia looked around the vast space. There were small clusters of people sipping her coffee and chatting amongst themselves. She noticed that the doorway where Tommy resided was perfectly in the centre of the units, looking out at the broken gate. Like a sheriff sitting on the porch of a small town police station in the Wild West, Julia doubted much got past this man.

"There's more people here than I imagined," Julia said, turning her attention back to Tommy as he shakily crammed the pink iced doughnut into his mouth. "I'm surprised the council isn't trying to do something to help."

Doughnuts and Deception

"Oh, they are," Tommy mumbled through a mouthful of doughnut. "They're doing plenty to help themselves. This place has been up for sale for redevelopment since the fire. The council is doing all they can to clear us lot away from here, but there's far too many to help rehouse and the shelters are bursting to capacity. They could arrest us all for squatting, but there aren't enough cells in the county. This doughnut is delicious by the way. You really do have a talent for baking."

"Thank you," Julia said. "So you're just staying here for as long as you can?"

"And then some," Tommy said, laughing as he licked his dirty fingers. "Developers are sniffing around everyday. It's only a matter of time before one of them takes the risk and puts in an offer. They'll level this place to the ground, stick some luxury apartments on here so those who can afford it will have somewhere nice to live."

"And those who can't are just left to move on somewhere else," Jessie jumped in. "It's sick."

"It's business," Tommy said with a heavy sigh. "It's not right, but it's how the world works. I should know. I used to be one of those developers."

"You were?" Julia asked, her brows shooting up.

"Oh, yes. Don't let my exterior fool you,"

Tommy said, winking out of the corner of his eye as he brushed the doughnut crumbs down the front of his threadbare jumper. "Before the recession hit, I was a landlord. I had a portfolio of a dozen properties. Then the banks collapsed and people stopped wanting to rent. It started small, but I couldn't afford the mortgages and I went bankrupt pretty quickly. I lost my career, my house, my wife, and everything in between."

"That's so sad," Julia said, bowing her head.

"It is what it is." Tommy shrugged, clearly already having let go of his past life. "Life has a funny way of working out like that. It's not all bad. Folks like you are always there to provide the coffee and doughnuts to those in need. There's a nice Christian couple, Stella and Max Moon who bring their soup truck here most nights." Tommy suddenly stood up and jutted his stick out in front of him, his lips snarling. "There's one of those rotten developers now!"

Julia looked to where Tommy was pointing his stick. A handsome, clean-shaven, well-groomed man in a sharp suit walked into the industrial park, followed by a team of almost identical looking men.

"That's Carl Black," Tommy spat through gritted teeth. "He's one of the worst. Doesn't even look at us like we're people. *Get out of here! Do you hear me?*"

Carl glanced in Tommy's direction but he barely registered a reaction. Julia caught the flicker of an amused smirk, making her instantly dislike the man. He reminded her of her ex-husband.

A couple of people joined in the jeering, some of them tossing their empty coffee cups in the direction of the men. The group behind Carl flinched, but Carl marched forward to the warehouse unbothered.

"There's a sense of community here, for the most part," Tommy said proudly. "We look after our own."

"The most part?" Julia asked, glancing to Jessie.

"Well, every community has its bad eggs," Tommy said, his bulging eyes darting around the crowd. "Take alcoholic Pete, for example. He's a drunk. Spends his days begging on the streets and every penny he gets, he spends on booze."

Julia followed Tommy's eyeline. A similarly aged man was leaning half asleep against a wall, a can of beer clutched tightly in his hands.

"And then there's the deaths," Tommy added.

"Deaths?"

"Dropping like flies recently," Tommy said, his

voice lowering as he leaned in. "It's what you expect in places like this, especially in the winter. All it takes is a cold night to get those older ones on the drink and drugs, but spring is upon us and people are still dying. Not your usual type, either. We had an eighteen-year-old die last week."

"Who?" Jessie asked, suddenly sitting up straight.

"Bailey Walker," Tommy said, dropping his head. "I know you were close to him, Jessie. I'm sorry. I was the one to find him. He was still in his sleeping bag past midday, but that wasn't like him. He was usually up and spraying his paint cans 'round the back. Helped him pass the day I think. So I went over and gave him a poke with my stick, and told him to get his lazy backside up, joking of course. But he didn't move. I pulled his sleeping bag back. He was as white as a sheet, so I sent one of the younger lads running to the phone box on the corner. Ambulance pronounced him dead and carted him away."

Julia placed a hand over her mouth, which had parted while listening to the story. She looked to Jessie, who was dabbing tears from the inside of her eyes with the edge of her sleeve.

"We were in the same foster house once," Jessie

said. "He got kicked out before I did. He was a good kid, he just – he just got into trouble a lot."

"What was the cause of death?" Julia asked, turning back to Tommy, who was looking sadly at Jessie.

"Inconclusive," Tommy said, his jaw gritting tightly. "They say it was a heart attack, but they don't know what caused it. At his age? Yeah, *right*. And he's not the only one. Remember the priest?"

"Father Thind?" Jessie asked, wiping away the last of her tears.

"Michael Thind." Tommy nodded. "He went two weeks after. Pete found him, dead in his sleeping bag, clutching his rosary beads. That man wouldn't have hurt a fly. And then there was Robert Culshaw, who went last week. Once again, in the sleeping bag. He used to be a banker in the city, but the recession hit him too."

Julia's mouth opened again. She looked around at the people surrounding her, wondering how many of them had lived relatively normal lives before ending up on the streets.

"Isn't somebody doing something?" Julia urged, edging closer to Tommy. "The police? They must be looking into it?"

"Three dead homeless people aren't enough to

even pique the police's interests," Tommy said with a bitter laugh. "They probably think they were druggies, or drunks. Don't get me wrong, when the sun sets and we all huddle around the fires, a couple of cans of beer get passed around, but those men didn't drink any more than the rest of us. Not enough to kill them."

"And there was nothing else to connect the men?" Julia asked.

"Aside from the fact they were men, there's nothing I know of," Tommy said, shaking his head. "Michael was in his fifties and Robert was in his forties. Those two kept to themselves. Like I said, it's not uncommon for people to die 'round here, but there's usually a reason. Healthy men, homeless or not, don't just die in their sleep."

"You're right," Julia said, pulling her ingredients notepad out of her handbag along with a small metal pen. "Can you give me those names again?"

After Julia had written down the names, they walked back to her car and packed away the equipment. Jessie said goodbye to Tommy and promised to visit soon. When the man hobbled back to his doorway, they jumped into the car and slowly drove out of Fenton Industrial Park.

"Why did you write down those names?" Jessie

asked, breaking the silence as they drove back to Peridale.

"I'm going to ask Barker if he knows anything," Julia said, looking straight ahead at the road as the cogs in her mind worked overtime. "There might be a perfectly reasonable explanation that the police haven't passed on."

"It is a little odd though, don't you think?" Jessie replied quietly as she chomped on her nails.

"It is more than a little odd," Julia agreed under her breath. "Very odd indeed."

CHAPTER 3

Peering over the top of her laptop, Julia looked through to the empty café. Jessie was standing behind the counter, scribbling something on a notepad, and the only customer, Julia's closest neighbour, Emily Burns, was pouring herself a second cup of tea from the pot. Julia liked the serenity of Monday mornings.

She usually used these quiet times to check her

stock levels and deep clean every corner of the kitchen, but this morning she was using it to surf the web. Looking back down at her computer, she picked up where she had left off reading an article about Bailey Walker's death in the *Cheltenham Standard*. The short article, which didn't contain a picture of the young boy, treated him as nothing more than a homeless statistic, whose cause of death was '*inconclusive*' but also '*non-suspicious*'.

She flicked between the three different newspaper articles she had been reading. Robert Culshaw, the ex-banker, was referenced as having two teenage daughters, but the emphasis was strongly on his status as a homeless man. There was a picture, which was credited as being pulled from the *Gloucestershire Bank* website, showing a smartly dressed, clean-shaven man with neatly cut hair. Julia wondered if the poor man had still looked like that when he was found dead. The third article, about Michael Thind's death, was a little more colourful. As well as a picture featuring him in his dog collar and black robes, the article went into detail about how Father Thind was fired after it was discovered he had been having an affair with another local clergyman. It then went on to describe the ins and outs of his messy divorce, which somehow lead to the man ending up on the streets.

"What are you doing?" Jessie asked, her sudden appearance startling Julia so much, she slapped her laptop shut. "I thought you were cleaning."

"I am," Julia said, her cheeks burning. "I was. I was just looking at something."

Jessie folded her arms and looked down her nose at the laptop, her eyes squinting tightly. Julia knew she had been rumbled.

"Wouldn't have anything to do with what Tommy said about those deaths, would it?" Jessie asked cautiously. "Because if you're investigating, I want to help."

"I'm not investigating."

"You investigated those other deaths," Jessie said, her arms tightening across her apron. "That organ lady and her son, and your father's brother-in-law. You investigated those and cracked the cases."

"It wasn't quite like that," Julia said, shaking her head. "I just – I was *just* looking online to cross-check what Tommy told us."

"You didn't believe him?"

"Of course I did," Julia said quickly. "I just wanted to be sure."

"Well?" Jessie urged, stepping forward and placing her hands on the other side of the metal preparation table. "What did you find?"

Julia sighed and opened her laptop. She hadn't wanted Jessie to know she was looking into things because she didn't want to get her hopes up. Things did seem odd, but Julia knew even the strangest things could have the simplest explanations. Jessie hurried to her side and pulled the laptop in front of her.

"There's not a lot of information in the articles," Julia said as she looked over Jessie's shoulder. "I was trying to find a link between them, but there isn't one that I can see. Aside from them all being men, and their causes of death being '*inconclusive*'."

"What does that mean?" Jessie asked, turning to stare at Julia expectantly.

"It means they didn't find a cause of death. Sometimes when people die, the cause isn't so obvious, so they do some tests, and if they can't find a reason, they rule it as an inconclusive cause of death."

"You mean they just couldn't be bothered?" Jessie snapped, pushing the laptop across the counter and turning to face Julia.

"They only look for certain things if they're suspicious. Sometimes people do just die and nobody knows why."

"But three men?" Jessie asked, her brows dropping low over her dark eyes. "You wouldn't be saying that if three men in this village suddenly died and nobody was trying to figure out why."

Jessie pushed angrily past Julia and burst through the beads, and back into the café. Julia hurried after her, wanting to explain, even if she didn't know what she was going to say. Julia knew Jessie was right. If three seemingly healthy men had died in Peridale in a short space of time, nobody would have accepted three '*inconclusive*' causes of death.

Julia pushed through the beads at the same time Barker walked into the café, clutching a wicker hamper. Without meaning to, Julia scowled at him, angry with herself for upsetting Jessie, who was furiously wiping down an already clean table. Julia looked desperately from her lodger to the Detective Inspector she had been dating for the last couple of weeks, wondering who she should give her attention to. Before she could make up her mind, Jessie decided for her and walked back through to the kitchen, leaving them alone in the café with Emily Burns, who could clearly sense the tension.

"Is this a bad time?" Barker asked with a strained smile as he walked towards the counter.

"It's fine," Julia lied, shaking out her curls and applying a smile. "What can I get you, Barker?"

"Actually, I was wondering if I could borrow you for half an hour?" Barker looked awkwardly down to the wicker hamper, which Julia realised was a picnic basket. "I took an early lunch and I wanted to treat you to a picnic on the village green."

Julia glanced over her shoulder to Jessie, who had resumed reading over the newspaper articles on the laptop screen. Julia turned back to Barker, who was smiling expectantly at her. Could she really turn him down?

"It's not really a good time," Julia said awkwardly. "Lots to do today."

"Oh," Barker said, frowning a little but retaining his smile. "I thought Mondays were always quiet? Unless you're expecting a sudden rush later?"

"We're not," Jessie said, suddenly appearing behind Julia. "I've got things covered here."

"Are you sure?" Julia asked, trying unsuccessfully to look into Jessie's eyes.

"Yep."

Julia reluctantly left her young lodger in charge of the café and followed Barker to the village green, which sat perfectly in the middle of Peridale. Barker laid down a red and white picnic blanket and Julia quickly sat in a position so that she could still see through her café window. Emily Burns appeared to be trying to coax some information out of Jessie, but Jessie didn't appear to be talking.

"Is something wrong?" Barker asked as he unloaded the picnic basket.

"Huh?" Julia mumbled, glancing to the food he had prepared. "I'm sorry, Barker. I'm just a little distracted."

"Well, if you can give me your attention for thirty minutes, I'll let you get back to being distracted." Barker smirked so sweetly, the butterflies in Julia's stomach danced unexpectedly, bringing her attention to the present.

"Deal," Julia said, sighing and shuffling across the blanket so that she was sitting next to Barker and couldn't look at her café. "Did you make all of this?"

"Ah," Barker said, smirking again. "Not quite. I was coming back from checking something out and passed a lovely looking sandwich shop."

"And the blanket and basket?"

"Borrowed them from the station's lost and found," Barker whispered. "Don't tell anyone. You'd never believe half of the stuff people hand in."

"Your secret is safe with me," Julia whispered back, her hair falling from behind her ear and over her face as she laughed gently.

Barker surprised her by reaching out and tucking the stray strand behind her ear. For a moment, the buzz of the village around them faded away as she looked into his eyes. She gulped, her throat suddenly dry. Laughing again, she turned her attention to the sandwiches as she felt her cheeks reddening.

"Bought or not, this all looks delicious," she said, her voice suddenly shaky.

Barker unwrapped tuna and cucumber, cheese and pickle, and egg and cress sandwiches, and laid them out on their foil wrappers on the blanket. Julia opted for a tuna and cucumber sandwich, not realising how hungry she was until she took her first bite. She had woken late that morning, and had had to rush through her Monday morning baking before opening the café, meaning she hadn't had time for her usual slice of toast and peppermint and liquorice tea.

Sitting under the early spring sun, with the hum of passing people and singing birds and buzzing insects, it was all so perfect, it made Julia forget about her café. When she finished her first half of her sandwich, she turned to Barker and shielded her eyes from the sun.

"This is our third date in a week," Julia said. "Anyone would think you were trying to court me, Detective Inspector."

"Wouldn't that be *quite* the scandal?" Barker joked, leaning in and lowering his voice. "You know the village has been talking about us."

"Let them," Julia whispered back. "It just shows that things have gone back to normal after these last couple of months of madness."

"Things have certainly calmed down," Barker agreed, before taking a bite of his sandwich, leaving behind the crust. "I spent my morning investigating a stolen tractor up at Peridale Farm. Yesterday, Amy Clark was convinced somebody had stolen her handbag, but she had just left it at bingo."

"Does it make you miss the city?"

Barker tossed his sandwich crust onto the foil and turned to Julia, shielding his eyes from the sun as it found its midday position in the clear blue sky.

"Not one bit," he said, smiling from ear to ear. "Besides, there are things in this village I never had in the city."

"Like?" Julia asked, her cheeks reddening again.

"Oh, you know," Barker said, shrugging softly. "Certain people."

Julia laughed and dropped her head again.

Doughnuts and Deception

When she looked up, her eyes locked with two dark circles poking out from the sitting room window of her gran's cottage.

"We're being watched," Julia said, nudging Barker with her shoulder.

Barker turned to look to where Julia was pointing. Julia realised the two dark circles belonged to a pair of binoculars being clutched by her gran. With them both looking in her direction, the lacy net curtains suddenly dropped back into their original position. The front door opened seconds later and Dot darted across the village green, her heavy binoculars bouncing under the brooch securing her blouse in place under her chin.

"Your gran scares me," Barker mumbled out of the corner of his mouth as Dot ran towards them.

"I'll tell her you said that," Julia mumbled back. "I think that's her goal."

Dot danced around a man walking his poodle, scowling down at the dog. When she finally made her way towards them, she slowed down and clutched her side, visibly out of breath.

"Afternoon, Gran," Julia called out. "Doing a spot of bird watching?"

"No," Dot said through her panting breaths. "Me and some of the girls have set up a neighbourhood watch group. Y'know, what with all of these recent murders and all."

"Nice to know my job is valued," Barker whispered under his breath.

"No *offence*, Detective Inspector," Dot said, her hearing much better than most people would think for a woman her age. "But if it wasn't for my Julia, there would still be two killers running around on the loose. Any of us could be next."

Julia held back her laughter. Her gran wasn't one to hold back, or spare on the dramatics. Barker on the other hand, was blushing and appeared lost for words. Julia knew her gran had just hit Barker where it hurt.

"What happened to your book club, Gran?" Julia asked, wanting to shift the conversation.

"Well," Dot said, taking it as an invitation to join them on the picnic blanket. "Some of the girls weren't too happy when we got to the mucky scenes in *Fifty Shades of Grey*. They didn't realise how filthy that Mr. Grey was. I quite enjoyed it myself. Are those egg and cress?"

Before either of them could respond, she reached out and plucked a sandwich from the mix. As she nibbled on the corner of the sandwich, Barker and Julia looked awkwardly at one another, neither appearing to know what to say.

"Seen anything interesting with those things?" Barker asked, a slight shake in his voice.

"The usual," Dot said. "I've been making notes. Hang on."

Dot reached into her breast pocket and pulled out a small notepad, not unlike the one Julia made her own notes in. She wondered if her gran was trying to investigate her own case so she could steal a little of the glory the rest of the village showered on Julia.

"*Eight-fifteen*. Julia and Jessie arrive at the café."

"Gran!" Julia said.

"You need protection!" Dot cried. "After what you went through when you caught Charles Wellington's killer, you need around the clock protection!"

Julia's fingers instinctively danced up to the fading scar on her forehead, which she had learned to conceal with her hair. It had only been two weeks since she had had the stitches removed, after being hit on the head with a recently boiled kettle while caught up in the middle of her father's brother-in-law's murder investigation. Her sister, Sue, was adamant Julia should talk to a surgeon to try and remove the scar, but Julia thought it added character.

"I'm fine, Gran," Julia said, trying to laugh. "Anything else?"

"*Ten-thirty-three.* A red tractor speeds through the village."

"A red tractor?" Barker jumped in. "Did you see who was driving it?"

"Of course I did!" Dot said, turning the page. "Billy Matthews."

"I knew it!" Barker said, snapping his fingers together. "That kid has been causing me trouble for weeks."

"See!" Dot said, stabbing her finger down on the pad. "I *told* you this was useful."

"And what use could you possibly have for spying on me and Barker eating lunch on the village green?" Julia asked, tilting her head quizzically at her gran.

"Well, you know," Dot fumbled over her words, flicking through the pages. "See here. Julia and Baker are having a date on the village green. *No* axe murderers in sight."

Julia and Barker both laughed. Julia was touched that her gran cared so much, although she was sure she was just spying to see how things were going. Dot had been trying to push their relationship along faster ever since Barker arrived in the village.

"Well, I'm flattered, Gran," Julia said. "But I'm a big girl and I can look after myself. Thanks for the sandwich, Barker, but I'm going to have to get back to the café."

"And me back to the station," he said, standing up and dusting the crumbs down his trousers. "I've got to visit the Fern More estate just out of the village. Billy Mathews' mother might like to know what her son has been up to."

"That estate has caused nothing but trouble since they built it!" Dot said as she peered through her binoculars at Roxy Carter, who was leaving the graveyard with her girlfriend, Violet Mason. "I protested to it being built in – what year was it? – Eighty-two? Are these sandwiches going begging?"

Barker held his hand out for Julia as Dot wrapped up the sandwiches and piled them under her arm. Julia attempted to help her gran up off the blanket but she brushed Julia's hand away and scrambled up to her feet on her own.

"Thanks for the sandwiches, Detective Inspector," Dot said as she turned and darted away. "Saved me a job for when the girls come around later to share notes."

They both watched as Dot walked back to her

cottage. The moment she was back inside, she resumed her position at the window, with her binoculars pushed through her lacy net curtains and up against the glass.

"Your gran is a character," Barker said as he packed away the blanket and basket. "One of these days we'll have an uninterrupted date."

"Oh, it's not so bad," Julia said, remembering their last date in a small country pub, which had been crashed by her sister and her husband. "If you add up all of these half-dates, we've almost had a full one somewhere along the way."

"Well, if you look at it like that," Barker said as they started to walk towards Julia's café. "I guess we have."

Outside the café, Julia peered through the window, where Jessie was serving Roxy and Violet. Jessie seemed a little happier, but her sadness was still obvious. Remembering what she had promised, Julia turned to Barker and pulled her own notepad out of her dress pocket. She flicked to a page she had specifically made for Barker and tore it out.

"Can you look into these names?" Julia asked, tucking the piece of paper into his pocket. "Three homeless men who frequented the Fenton Industrial Park have died recently, all without any real identifiable cause of death. Could you see if there's anything else out there that hasn't been passed onto the press? They were friends of Jessie's and it would mean a lot to her."

"I'll see what I can find," Barker said, tapping the pocket. "You're not – *investigating* again, are you?"

"My days of investigating are behind me," Julia said with a wink as she turned around and pulled open her café door. "Besides, my gran's got that covered now. See you later, Detective Inspector."

CHAPTER 4

With even more doughnuts and coffee, Julia and Jessie returned to Fenton Industrial Park after sunset that night. The tension from their butting of heads in the café earlier had blown over, leaving behind only a slight undercurrent.

"This is far too kind of you," Tommy said, licking his lips after finishing his doughnut. "We've never been as well fed as these last two days. They're going to start hailing you as our lord and saviour soon enough. You watch!"

After everyone was fed and Julia's equipment was locked safely in her car, they headed over to Tommy's doorway, where the two upturned baskets were still positioned from the day before.

"Julia has talked to her detective boyfriend," Jessie said quickly, nibbling on the edges of her nails. "He's going to look into it."

"Is that right?" Tommy murmured, a brow suspiciously arching.

"Well, not quite," Julia corrected Jessie, smiling awkwardly at Tommy. "I gave him the names and I asked him to see if he could find something. Unofficially, that is."

"Sounds about right," Tommy said, shaking his head heavily. "The police don't care if we live or die."

Julia wanted to tell him that wasn't true, but she looked over her shoulder at the dozens of people crowding around various fires, wrapped up in their half a dozen layers of clothing each. Her doughnuts and coffee seemed to have brought smiles to some of the downturned faces, but it was like putting a single stitch over a bullet hole. There was a bigger issue at play here, and the police and the government weren't doing enough. Her heart ached knowing this was where Jessie had been living before she took her into her home.

"I wanted to ask you if there's anything else you knew about the men who died," Jessie said, turning her attention back to Tommy as he clutched his plastic cup of coffee for warmth, his dirty nails poking out of his fingerless gloves. "You said you found Bailey. I was just wondering if you noticed anything *suspicious*."

"Like I told you yesterday, ma'dear, I thought he was asleep and then I realised he was dead, so we called for the ambulance and the police. That's all I know."

"And the others?" Jessie asked, edging forward on her basket. "Who found them?"

"Mac found Father Thind, and alcoholic Pete found Robert," Tommy said, tossing a finger in Pete's direction as he stumbled from group to group, a can of beer firmly in his hands. "Although you won't get much from him. His mind has gone. Thinks everything is a conspiracy and aliens are coming to take him away."

"And Mac?" Julia asked.

"He's that young lad in the corner playing the

guitar," Tommy said, tossing a finger across the car park. "Talented kid. American."

Julia excused herself and left Jessie with Tommy. Stuffing her fingers into the pockets of her pale pink peacoat, she approached the man as he strummed away on his guitar to an invisible audience. Leaning over his instrument, his shaggy dark hair covered his face as he played, unaware of Julia's presence. She held back and listened for a moment as his fingers delicately danced over the strings, creating a soft melody that transported her out of the urban and stark surroundings. Tommy was right, the man was talented. How could somebody with such a gift be living in such as Fenton Industrial Park?

"You play so beautifully," Julia said as she stepped forward. "Do you mind if I take a seat?"

The man looked up from under his messy hair, and his beauty caught Julia off-guard. She had been expecting somebody older and more rugged, but a soft, slightly tanned face stared up at her, his crystal blue eyes filled with as much melody as his music.

"Not at all," Mac said, the thickness of his American accent taking her by surprise. "It's always nice to have a beautiful lady to play for."

Aware that she was blushing, Julia perched herself on the edge of the upturned crate in front of

Mac. He continued his playing as he looked into her eyes. The music wrapped around Julia like a warm blanket. She almost forgot why she had come to talk to the man in the first place.

"How long have you played?" Julia asked, hypnotised by the intricacy and speed of his fingers.

"For as long as I can remember," Mac said, smiling to reveal his dazzling white teeth. "It's the only thing keeping me sane."

"You could play professionally," Julia offered as Mac stopped playing and rested the guitar next to him, leaning his arm on top of the headstock.

"I did," Mac said, his smile wavering a little, but his gaze not breaking away from Julia. "The music industry is a fickle place, lady. I came over with the promise of a deal, but things don't always work out the way you plan."

"What about home?" Julia asked. "America?"

"Minnesota," he said with a nod. "There's as much for me there as here. My folks died when I was little and I was an only child. As long as I have my guitar, and people like you to appreciate my music, I'm a happy man. I have clothes on my back, and people like you who are kind enough to keep putting doughnuts in my stomach."

Julia waited for his gaze to waver, but it didn't.

Doughnuts and Deception

She actually believed that he was happy. His life was simple and his needs were as basic as a person's got, but his smile was as genuine as a man with all of the money in the world.

"Can I ask you something?" Julia asked. "Something a little *sensitive*."

"Go ahead, lady. As long as it's something I want to answer."

"It's about Robert Culshaw," Julia said, her lips trembling a little. "The banker? Tommy told me you were the one who found him when he -,"

"Was murdered?"

"So you believe it was murder?"

"Of course I do," Mac said, leaning back and looking suspiciously at Julia. "All the folks in these parts do. The man was as clean as they come. The others, I could understand, but not Robert."

"Clean?"

"Y'know," Mac said, nodding his head suggestively at Julia. "Alcohol and drugs. I'm not saying the others weren't clean. I didn't know them all that well, but Robert was a healthy man. He wouldn't just die for no damn reason."

Mac ran his hands down his face, his smile dropping for the first time. It was obvious the death of his friend had hit him hard.

"Is there anything you can tell me about the night you found him?" Julia asked softly, not wanting to upset the young musician. "Anything out of the ordinary that you noticed?"

"I was busking on the high street all afternoon. It was a Saturday, so people were generous with their tips. By the time the police moved me on, I had enough for a couple of drinks in the pub, so I took my cash and my guitar and I pitched up in a dark corner and had a couple of pints. Not many, just enough to keep me warm for the rest of the night. I stayed there until they closed because it was somewhere dry. It was raining that night, so when I got back, everybody was huddled up inside the burnt out buildings. We don't usually go in there much because it's not safe. Wind hits that place in the right direction and huge chunks of the roof cave in. I was running across the car park to the building when I saw Robert in his sleeping bag. He always slept in the same place, every night, unless it was raining. I wondered if he'd had some drinks too and he didn't realise it was raining, so I went over to wake him. His eyes and mouth were open and he was blue. I knew he was dead. I ran to the phone box on the corner and I dialled 999. I didn't notice anything else because his sleeping bag was zipped all the way up to his neck. That's the last I saw of him."

Mac suddenly broke off and looked down, his clasped hands pressed tightly against his lips. Julia reached out and rested her hand on the young man's shoulder, giving it a reassuring squeeze. He looked up and smiled appreciatively, appearing to be holding back his tears.

"Can you show me where he was sleeping when you found him?" Julia asked. "Maybe there's something the police missed."

"I thought the cops back home were a joke, but yours really do – what's the expression? *Take the biscuit?* It was just over there next to that empty gas canister."

Mac cast a finger along the metal fence to a spot only a couple of feet away. Thanking him for his help, she walked over to the red, upturned canister next to the fence. She scanned the ground, but there were no signs of anything out of the ordinary. She imagined the poor man dead in his sleeping bag and her chest tightened. Closing her eyes for a moment, she inhaled deeply before looking over her shoulder to Jessie and Tommy. They were both deep in conversation, huge smiles on their faces.

Julia looked ahead through the fence panels. An unlit path ran along the side of the industrial park, winding out of view. Pushing her hands up against the fence, she tried to see where it went. As she did, the metal slats moved under her touch. She jumped back, and frowned at the fence. She ran her fingers along the panels. All of them were securely in place, apart from two that had been unscrewed at the bottom. Parting the slats, she pushed her leg through, and then her torso. Julia wasn't a big woman, but she was fifteen to twenty pounds above average, depending on the time of year. She slipped through the opening in the fence with ease.

"Are you making a bid for freedom?" Tommy asked, startling her.

Julia slid back through the fence and crouched down to look at the missing bolts that allowed the fence panels to move. She ran her fingers along the holes, noticing how fresh the metal underneath looked. It appeared as though the bolts hadn't been missing for long.

"How long has this fence been like this?" Julia asked Tommy, who was standing behind her with Jessie.

"Is it important?" Jessie looked down her nose at Julia as she examined the ground around the fence.

"I don't know," Julia mumbled, tapping her chin. "Maybe. Maybe not."

"I couldn't tell you, truth be told," Tommy said with a frown as he leaned his entire bodyweight on his stick. "Why do you ask?"

"Where was Bailey when you found him?" Julia asked, pushing herself up from the ground and brushing the creases out of her peacoat.

"Just here," Tommy said, walking a couple of feet down the fence and tapping his stick on the ground. "He was facing into the fence. What are you thinking, Julia?"

"Nothing," Julia said, forcing forward a smile, not wanting to give Tommy false hope. "I'm just overthinking things."

"There's a soup van," Jessie said, hooking her thumb over her shoulder to a food truck that had pulled up outside of the entrance of the industrial park. "Stella and Max from the soup kitchen always bring their leftovers at this time of night and there's always plenty to go around."

"Sounds good to me," Julia said with a nod. "Lead the way."

As they joined the end of the long line for soup, Julia glanced over her shoulder at the fence, knowing it was more than possible for somebody to sneak in during the night to kill homeless people. Looking at Mac as he strummed away peacefully on his guitar, she wondered what could possibly motivate somebody to do such a terrible thing.

CHAPTER 5

L ater that week, Julia found herself sitting at Barker's dining room table for a second attempt of their ruined picnic date. The bought sandwiches were gone, replaced with the rich and hearty scent of beef stew drifting through from the kitchen as Barker topped up their wine glasses.

"I see you've unpacked," Julia said, motioning through the archway to the living room, which had still been full of boxes on her last visit. "It's starting to feel a little homelier around here."

"Well, I figured if I was sticking around in the village I had to stop living out of boxes." Barker sipped his wine, his eyes twinkling in the flickering candlelight. "I'd like to think I've put my own touch on the place."

Julia looked around the cottage, which was still quite bare compared to her own. The furniture was white and sterile, more suited to a city apartment than a Cotswold cottage. That juxtaposition matched Barker's presence in the village, but both seemed to work.

Barker hurried off to the kitchen and returned with two large bowls filled to the brim with rich, bubbling beef stew. He had splashed the gravy all down the sides of the white bowl, and slapped the dish on the table without a placemat. It wasn't exactly how Julia would do things, but she appreciated the effort all the same.

"This smells delicious for a man who claimed not to be able to cook," Julia said as she leaned into the steaming bowl.

"This is one of the few things my old mum taught me," Barker said as he topped up their already full wine glasses again. "You fry some onions and garlic, toss in some bacon and beef, add the stock, a glug or three of red wine, and then you throw the whole thing in a slow cooker for the best part of a day. Idiot proof!"

Julia skimmed her spoon across the top of the stew and sampled Barker's creation. It tasted as delicious as it smelled, and the red wine definitely shone through.

"Tell me more about your mother," Julia asked as they started to tuck into their food. "You've never spoken about her before."

Barker smiled sadly down into his stew. Just from the slight crease between his brows, she could sense that Barker's mother was in the same place as her own.

"She died five years ago," Barker said, dropping his spoon and leaning across the table towards Julia. "She was a remarkable woman. She swore like a sailor but she had a heart of gold. She wasn't a woman many people would dare cross, because she would let them know about it. She raised me and my brothers singlehandedly and she never once complained."

"I'm sad I couldn't meet her. She sounds great."

"She would have loved you," Barker said with a warm smile, his eyes sparkling. "She had a sweet tooth like nobody I've ever met, so you two would have gotten on like a house on fire."

"What was her favourite cake?"

"She could never say no to a coconut cake," Barker said with a small sigh. "I haven't had one since her funeral. The whole buffet at the funeral was cakes. We knew she would have loved that."

Julia made a mental note to dig through her own mother's handwritten recipe books because she was sure she had come across a coconut cake recipe in her time. Barker was more of a double chocolate cake type of man, but she knew it would bring a smile to his face. She liked hearing about his life, even if it did make her realise how little she knew the village's new Detective Inspector.

"Are you close to your brothers?" Julia asked, already feeling full but barely making a dent in her overflowing stew.

"As close as a group of men with their own careers can be,'" Barker said, pausing to sip his wine. "I'm the baby of four, and I'm the only bachelor in the family, which only becomes more apparent at family parties. They've all got wives and between them they've given me nine nieces and nephews. Keeps Christmas expensive."

"Have you never thought about having kids?"

Doughnuts and Deception

"I did," Barker said with a firm nod. "Once upon a time."

Julia sensed some sadness in his words. Were they connected to a previous relationship? She almost asked, but she bit her tongue, remembering she still hadn't told Barker that she was technically still in the middle of her divorce. She had finally signed her papers and sent them off to her solicitor, but she was still waiting to hear if their decree absolute had been granted. Jerrad had been the one pushing the process along ever since changing the locks of their London apartment and politely informing her he was leaving her for his twenty-seven-year-old secretary, but she wouldn't put it past him to start dragging his heels in the final stages. She decided that was a can of worms better left sealed.

"What about you?" Barker asked. "Do you see kids on the horizon?"

The question caught Julia off guard. As a young woman, she had just assumed she would one day have a big family, but like Barker, it just hadn't worked out that way.

"I don't know," Julia answered honestly. "Life has a funny way of throwing things at you, don't you think? I certainly never expected to be fostering a teenager, or dating a Detective Inspector."

"What you've done with Jessie is an amazing thing," Barker said sincerely. "You should be really proud of yourself. Not many would be as understanding as you have been. How's the fostering process going?"

"Slow," Julia said, pushing her half-finished bowl away from her. "They've granted me temporary fostering rights because she's a young adult and settled, but it's a slow process. We're still waiting for anything official."

"What about when she turns eighteen?" Barker asked, copying Julia and pushing away his barely touched stew. "What are you going to do with her?"

"She's not an old couch," Julia replied coolly, arching a brow. "I'm not just going to kick her out."

"I wouldn't expect you to." Barker held up his hands before topping up their wine again.

"I suppose I'll let Jessie decide what she wants to do. My guest bedroom isn't going anywhere, and neither is my café, so I'm here for her as long as she wants me."

"You're a good woman, Julia," Barker smiled softly over the rim of his wine glass. "If the world was filled with more Julias, it would be a better place."

"I'm nothing special," Julia mumbled, ruffling

her hair as she felt her cheeks blush. "I'm just a plain old baker."

"You're anything but plain, Julia. You're so much more than that."

Julia smiled and met Barker's eyes through the candlelight. He reached out and rested his hand upon hers. It was such a simple action, but it caused such an extraordinary reaction within Julia. A rush of fire shot up her arm and spread rapidly within her body, causing the baby hairs on the back of her neck to prickle.

"Why don't we take this wine through to the living room?" Barker asked, already standing. "The couch might be a little comfier."

Julia attempted to reply, but she suddenly had a frog in her throat. She coughed and nodded, scooping up her wine glass. She followed Barker through to the dimly lit living room and they sat next to each other on the couch. He leaned forward and using a long lighter, he lit three untouched candles in a glass stand on the clutter-free coffee table.

"Quite ingenious to have a date in my cottage," Barker said, darting his brows up and down. "No worry of being interrupted."

Julia coughed again and gulped down her wine

quickly. Red wine wasn't her favourite, but it had been a long and busy week and it was taking the edge off. Every time she was with Barker, she felt inexplicably nervous, something she had never felt with Jerrad. When she had explained this to Sue, her sister had been adamant those feelings were love, but Julia was sure it was too soon to feel something so strong.

"It's been a lovely evening," Julia said, perching on the edge of the couch. "You should cook more often. You're quite good at it."

"I'll take that as a compliment," Barker chuckled softly, spreading his arm across the back of the leather couch. "You'll have to teach me some of your cake recipes. Something simple to get me started."

Barker's fingers suddenly danced across the back of Julia's arms, resting on her shoulder. Her body stiffened, but she couldn't deny she liked the feeling of Barker's hands on her. Sipping her wine, she allowed herself to lean into his masculine chest.

"A Victoria sponge cake is always a good place to start," she said, the shake in her voice obvious. "Or a classic scone."

"Sounds delicious," Barker said, looking down into her eyes. "You're a kind woman, Julia. I really like you."

Doughnuts and Deception

"I like you too, Detective Inspector."

"No," Barker said softly, shaking his head a little as he laughed. "I *really* like you."

Barker rested his glass of red wine on the square couch arm and hooked his finger under Julia's chin. They stared deeply into each other's eyes, their faces so close she could smell Barker's musky aftershave on his neck. Gulping, she blinked slowly, noticing that she was edging closer to his lips.

"I really like you too," Julia whispered, her fingers clutching the wine glass so tightly she was sure it was about to shatter.

Barker's hand slid from her chin, to the side of her face, his fingers touching the edge of her hair and his palm cupping her cheek. She closed her eyes, smiling as Barker's soft lips and stubbly chin brushed against her.

She didn't have time to savour the moment because a sudden banging at the door startled them both. Barker jumped back, knocking his red wine and drenching the front of his crisp, white shirt. Cursing out, he stood up and let the wine drip to the white fluffy rug under the glass coffee table. It almost resembled blood.

"Who's that at this time of night?" Barker mumbled angrily as he headed into the hallway, flicking wine off his hands.

Julia placed her own wine on the table and stood up, observing herself in the mirror above the fireplace. Her hair was a little ruffled, her berry-tinted lips were slightly smudged from Barker's kiss, and her eyes were a little blurry from the never-ending glass of red wine. Julia had barely finished straightening herself up before Jessie burst into the room.

"Tommy just called," Jessie said gravely, staring deep into Julia's eyes, thankfully not seeming to notice what she had just interrupted. "Somebody else has just died. We need to get there now."

"I've been drinking," Julia said reactively. "We both have."

"I'll call a taxi," Barker said, appearing behind Jessie. "Let me go and change my shirt and I'll be right back."

Barker rushed past them both and along the hallway to his bedroom. Through a crack in the door, Julia watched as Barker pulled off his stained shirt. Shaking her head, she turned her attention back to Jessie.

"Do you know who has died?" Julia asked, resting her hand on her forehead as she attempted to steady her thoughts.

Doughnuts and Deception

"Mac," Jessie said darkly, her bottom lip trembling. "The guitar guy."

CHAPTER 6

The taxi ride to Fenton Industrial Park was a long and uncomfortable one. Barker sat in the front seat, slapping the dashboard every time they stopped at a traffic light, demanding loudly that the taxi driver speed through them. Despite Barker flashing his badge at the driver more than once, the man barely registered any acknowledgement.

Doughnuts and Deception

In the back seat, Julia held Jessie as she sobbed silently, dampening Julia's shoulder. She stroked the girl's back, trying her best to soothe her. The more she focussed on Jessie's tears, the easier it was to hold back her own. She had only talked to the musician at the beginning of the week. She couldn't believe such a talented young man with a staunchly positive outlook on his bleak situation was no longer among the living. She couldn't wrap her head around the injustice.

When they pulled up outside the industrial park behind two parked police cars, Barker didn't wait for the taxi to stop before he tossed the money at the driver and jumped out. Julia apologised on his behalf, but once again, the driver barely flinched.

Practically cradling Jessie, Julia helped her out of the car. Two paramedics walked by carrying a stretcher wrapped in a red blanket, so she clasped Jessie's head to her chest to shield her from seeing such a thing. Julia, on the other hand, couldn't look away. As they put the Mac's body into the back of the ambulance, a tear rolled down her cheek when she saw his dark, scruffy hair poking out.

"Jessie!" Tommy cried, hobbling out of the industrial park. "Oh, you poor thing. Come here."

Jessie let go of Julia and ran into the old man's

arms. Balancing on his stick, he wrapped his free arm around her and rested his cheek on her head as he stroked the back of her hair.

"What happened, Tommy?" Julia asked, resting her hand on the old man's shoulder.

"It's the same exact thing," Tommy yelled, casting his stick towards the fence where Barker was talking to two uniformed officers. "Those pigs won't listen to me! They don't care if we live or die!"

Julia set off towards Barker, her stomach knotting when she saw Mac's guitar lying on the floor in the corner where she had listened to him playing only days ago, its neck broken, and half of its strings snapped.

"He's been dead a good twelve hours," she heard one of the officers tell Barker. "There's nothing to suggest any foul play. You know what it's like with these people."

Barker grumbled a reply but he didn't correct the officer. He walked around to the sleeping bag, pulling it open a little and peering inside.

"And this is where you found him?" Barker asked, letting go of the sleeping bag and standing back up. "In his sleeping bag?"

"If you ask me, boss, he was a junkie like the rest of them and took it too far," the other officer said.

"They're dropping like flies."

"He wasn't on drugs," Julia said, clearing her throat and stepping forward. "I spoke to him a couple of days ago and he told me he didn't touch them. He was a guitar player."

"Aren't you a little dressed up to be homeless, love?" one of the officers said, smirking as he looked her up and down.

"I'm not homeless," Julia said sternly, pursing her lips and planting her hands on her hips. "Did you know he is the fourth man to die in this exact same place in the last month?"

"I was aware of that," the older officer said, hooking his thumbs into his belt and cocking his head back. "But none of them died suspiciously as far as we're concerned."

"You're telling me there's nothing suspicious about four men dying, three of whom with inconclusive causes of death, and if I had to bet on it, a fourth one to be added to that same list?" Julia walked over to the fence and touched the moveable panels. "If you ask me, that's the most suspicious thing I think I've ever heard."

"Well, nobody asked you, love," the younger officer snickered, rolling his eyes at Barker. "Get out of here."

"Don't talk to her like that," Barker said firmly, his jaw flinching. "Julia, go and wait with Jessie."

The two officers suddenly straightened up and tossed their gazes to the ground.

"Somebody needs to take this seriously, Barker," Julia pleaded. "This is beyond coincidence now. Three men might have been able to slide, but *four*? I'd bet my café that these men were murdered."

The older officer sighed heavily, rolling his eyes at the younger officer, his head still dropped. Julia was used to members of the police force underestimating her.

"These fence panels move," Julia said, undeterred by the officers. "I know for a fact that three of the men all died up and down this fence. My theory is that whoever is murdering these men, they're squeezing through this gap in the fence and somehow killing them while they sleep."

"And how do you suppose they're doing that?" the younger officer sneered, barely holding back his laughter. "The kiss of death? These men weren't strangled, smothered, or stabbed. There's no cause of death. And besides, that gap is tiny. Only a tiny woman or child would fit through there."

Julia grabbed hold of the young officer's arm and pulled him towards the fence. Reaching over the tall man, she pried apart the metal panels and pushed him through. The front of his uniform snagged the metal, but he fit.

"*Alright*, lady," the officer cried, pulling himself free of Julia and pushing down his jacket. "I get your point. Tell me this then, Sherlock. Why would anybody want to kill random homeless people in their sleep?"

"Because the human condition isn't predictable or logical, officer," Julia said calmly, making sure to retain the sceptic's gaze. "The question here shouldn't be why, but how. How are these poor, innocent men being murdered, and what are you doing to catch whoever it is before a fifth man is discovered?"

Both officers looked at each other, each of them seemingly lost for words. The older officer's jaw flapped, but he didn't speak. Out of the corner of her eye, she caught Barker smirking. Before either of them answered, a call came in over the radio and they doubled back, shaking their heads as they walked away.

"You know he could have arrested you for pushing him through a fence like that?" Barker said. "Technically, you just assaulted an officer of the law."

"I know," she said, shrugging and staring firmly at the men as they walked towards the exit. "Technically, those men are idiots."

"I couldn't have protected you if they carted you off to the station," Barker whispered into her ear as they followed the officers towards the gate.

"I can look after myself, Detective Inspector," Julia said. "If the police aren't going to take this seriously, somebody has to, and if that person has to be me, so be it."

Barker shook his head and pinched between his brows. He let out a heavy sigh, but he didn't try to dissuade her. They both knew nothing he could say could make her back down.

"Do you know who found him?" Julia asked Tommy, who was sitting on the edge of the kerb with Jessie where the ambulance had been. "I'd like to speak to them."

"Cindy," Tommy said, hobbling to his feet with Jessie's help. "She's at Stella and Max's soup kitchen a couple of miles away. They were here with their food truck when she found him so they went and opened up especially for them. Most followed on, but I hung back to wait for you."

"I'll call a taxi," Julia said as she dug in her handbag for her phone. "I'll make sure to call a different one, Barker. I don't think that driver would appreciate seeing you again."

CHAPTER 7

Stella and Max Moon's soup kitchen was tucked away on a dark backstreet, sandwiched between a boarded up nightclub and a twenty-four hour off-license. Just like Fenton Industrial Park, it was tucked away on the outskirts of town, hidden from view.

"They're good people," Tommy said as they all climbed out of the taxi. "Good Christian people."

Doughnuts and Deception

"I didn't even know places like this existed out here," Barker mumbled, almost under his breath. Julia detected the tinge of guilt in his voice.

"Most people don't," Jessie replied flatly. "That's the problem."

Inside of the soup kitchen, an eerie silence clouded the air. Groups of people sat around tables, some of them whispering, some of them rolling cigarettes and drinking from beer cans, but most were staring blankly ahead. Julia sensed their fear and hopelessness.

"We need to help these people," Julia whispered to Barker as they followed Tommy across the vast space. "This can't happen again."

"Let's just see what this woman says," he whispered back, resting his hand in the small of her back. "It'll be okay."

Julia wanted to believe him, but she wasn't sure. The more time she spent in this world, the more she realised how ignored and disregarded the people living in it were. At the end of the day, she could go home to her warm cottage, take a hot bath, and sleep in a comfortable bed. She had never felt more grateful for her privilege than she had in the last week.

"Cindy?" Tommy said quietly as he approached

a table where a nervous looking woman sat. "Can we sit down?"

"Free country," she said, sniffling and wiping her nose with the back of her hand. "Who are the well dressed folks?"

"These are my friends," Tommy said, smiling at Julia, who in turn smiled at Cindy. "You remember Jessie, don't you? Julia here has taken her into her home, and this is her boyfriend, Barker. He's a Detective."

"Detective Inspector," Barker corrected him. "And I'm not here on official business."

They sat at the table as Cindy tucked her scraggly blonde hair behind her ears. Julia would have guessed they were similar ages, but years on the street had taken their toll on the woman. Her eyes were sunken, her teeth were stained, and her nose was red raw.

"Tommy told me you found Mac," Julia said softly, leaning across the table to Cindy. "That must have been difficult."

"I told the police all I know," she snapped back, tucking her bony knees up into her chest and clutching them with her hands. "I don't know nuffin'. I just thought he was sleeping. I went to wake him up, to see if he had any money. He was good like that. He always gave me a couple of quid to get some cans or whatever. He'd been sleeping all day, but that's not unusual, y'know? There's not much else to do. I've never been a good sleeper myself. My mam used to say I'd wake if the wind changed direction. I put my hand on him, but he didn't move. He was stiff as a board. I pulled back his sleeping bag and I knew he was dead. Not the first body I've seen. Probably won't be the last either, if you know what I'm saying?"

"Did you see anything suspicious?" Julia asked.

"I told the police what I told them," she said again, wiping her runny nose with the back of her hand. "I said to them that I saw marks on his arm, but I told them, I said '*Mac doesn't touch the drugs*'. He wasn't like that. He was a good kid."

Julia looked down at the woman's arms as she scrambled to tuck her hair behind her ears. She noticed tiny red marks littering the inside of her forearm. She glanced to Barker and he seemed to have noticed them too, and they both appeared to think the same thing at the same time; whatever she told them couldn't be guaranteed to be entirely reliable.

"She's right," Tommy said. "Mac was clean. He was against all of that stuff."

"Are you sure you saw some marks on his arm?" Julia asked, lowering her voice and leaning in. "Absolutely sure?"

"I saw what I *saw*, lady."

Julia pulled back, glancing awkwardly at Barker, who shrugged. At that moment, Stella Moon walked over and placed a plate of pale golden toast smothered in butter on the table. Cindy dove in immediately.

"We didn't have any ingredients for soup left, so I tossed some bread in the toaster," Stella said softly, clutching the tiny silver crucifix around her neck. "How are you feeling, Cindy?"

"Sad," Cindy said as she crammed a second slice of toast into her already full mouth. "Hungry."

Stella smiled sadly at the woman before turning and heading back to the counter, where her husband, Max, was opening a new loaf of bread. Stella appeared to be in her early forties, but she dressed like a woman more like Julia's gran's age. She was wearing a pleated calf-length skirt, a lilac cardigan, and thick, clumpy shoes. Her long mousy brown hair was scraped off her make-up free face in a loose ponytail at the base of her neck. Unstylish, functional glasses balanced on the edge of her slender nose. Aside from the small crucifix on a simple chain around her neck, she wasn't wearing any jewellery.

"Somebody murdered him, if you ask me," Cindy mumbled through a mouthful of toast. "Injected something into him."

"It's the government," the man, who Tommy had referred to as 'alcoholic Pete' said, staggering towards their table with a can of beer clutched in his hand. "They're experimenting on us. Testing a new super virus."

"Leave off, Pete," Tommy cried, rolling his eyes heavily.

"It's true!" Pete cried, slapping his hands on the table and sloshing his beer on Julia's dress. "You heard the lady. Puncture marks. Mac wasn't like that, and neither was the priest."

Julia remembered what Tommy had told her about Pete finding Michael Thind's body. She hadn't been brave enough to approach Pete to ask him questions, but now that he was here volunteering information, drunk or not, she knew it was her chance to ask questions.

"Did you find puncture marks on Father Thind?" Julia asked.

"What's it to you?" Pete slurred, pointing in Julia's face and glancing up and down her body.

"Make it worth my while?"

Barker pulled out his wallet and slapped a twenty pound note on the table and pushed it towards Pete. Pete and Cindy's eyes lit up.

"Tell the woman what you know," Barker said.

"He had three holes in his arm," Pete said sternly, tucking the note deep in his pockets. "Looked like somebody was trying to find a vein."

"And you don't think it was Michael doing that to himself?" Barker asked.

"He was a man of God!" Cindy replied. "'Course not."

"Michael was as straight edge as they came," Pete offered, leaning against the table. "Wouldn't even touch booze. I told him he was missing out, but he wouldn't listen. I told the police this but they didn't listen either."

"I'm not surprised," Tommy muttered bitterly. "Clear off, Pete."

"I'm talking to the *nice* lady," Pete cried, sloshing his can in Tommy's direction. "*Not* you, old man."

Tommy mumbled something under his breath before standing up and hobbling across the canteen to another table.

"Old fool thinks he runs things," Pete said.

Doughnuts and Deception

"He's not so squeaky clean."

"Don't you say a bad word against him!" Jessie said, jumping up.

"The prodigal daughter returns," Pete sneered. "And here I was thinking the aliens had got you too."

Jessie rolled her eyes and joined Tommy on the other table. They both glanced over their shoulder, glaring at Pete.

"Are you sure you saw puncture marks?" Julia asked, eager to get back on track.

"I'm sure," Pete said firmly. "The government injected him with something, just like the others. They're trying to wipe us out, but we won't go down without a fight."

"Why would the government want to kill homeless people?" Barker asked, clearly not taking Pete seriously.

"To get rid of us," Pete said, as though it was an obvious answer. "They've been trying to get rid of us for years. I'm going outside for a ciggie. Are you coming, Cindy?"

Cindy nodded, cramming the last slice of toast into her mouth. She untucked her knees and scurried out of her seat, following Pete towards the door. Julia turned to Barker, but it was clear they weren't on the same page.

"Please tell me you don't believe any of that, do you?" Barker asked with a heavy sigh, clearly wanting to laugh. "It's the ramblings of a drunk. Neither of them can be believed."

"What if they're on the right track?" Julia asked, lowering her voice and leaning in. "The whole bit about the government and the aliens is nonsense, but what if they're right about the injections? I spoke to Mac myself and I saw him with my own two eyes. He wasn't on drugs. What if this is the cause of death?"

"Lethal injection?" Barker asked, pursing his lips. "But why?"

"I don't know that yet, but this is the best lead we have."

"You're talking like a detective," Barker said, smirking a little.

"Somebody has to," Julia said, glancing over to Jessie. "You saw how little those officers cared. Somebody has to do something. You have to admit things don't add up."

"They don't," Baker agreed. "But there's not a lot I can do. If these deaths are being ruled as non-suspicious, it's going to be difficult for anyone to try and get somebody in the force to listen. The last thing any of them want is to admit that there might be a serial killer out there."

"We don't need the force," Julia said. "No offence."

"None taken."

"We can crack this, Barker." Julia reached out and grabbed his hands in hers. "You and me. The minute we have something concrete, you can take it to your boss and be the hero."

"It's not about that, Julia. I'm worried about you."

"I'll be fine," she said quickly, letting go of his hands.

"You always say that but you have a habit of putting yourself in danger, and it scares me."

"Don't worry about me," Julia said as she peered around the full canteen. "It's these people we need to worry about. Are you in?"

Barker exhaled heavily through his nose. He looked around the canteen, his eyes pausing on Jessie as she chatted with Tommy. He turned back to Julia and picked up her hands.

"I'll do what I can," Barker said. "Within the law."

"That's good enough for me," Julia said, concealing her smile as she stood up. "Go and make sure Jessie is okay. I'm going to talk to Sally and Max. They're at the industrial park a lot and they might have seen something."

"Why do I feel like you've just become my boss?"

"You say that like it's a bad thing," Julia whispered, winking as she turned around.

Julia left Barker and walked over to the counter where Stella and Max were buttering fresh slices of toast. They both looked up and smiled meekly at Julia as she leaned against the counter and waited for them to finish.

"You're the doughnuts and coffee lady, aren't you?" Stella asked, peering over her glasses at Julia with a soft smile. "It's nice to see another Christian woman."

"Oh, I'm not Christian," Julia corrected her. "I don't think so anyway. I believe in something, I think, I'm just not quite sure."

"God is all around," Max said, smiling in the same soft way as he buttered the final slice of toast. "There are many roads to Him. Just because you don't put the label on it, doesn't mean you don't believe."

"Maybe," Julia said. "I just wanted to say that I really admire what you both do for these people."

Doughnuts and Deception

"We're doing what we can to make the world a better place," Stella said, putting down the butter knife and opening the door to the kitchen. "Come through."

Julia thanked her and walked into the brightly lit kitchen. It was three times bigger than her own café's kitchen, and she couldn't help but think how much easier it would be to bake in such a space, even if it was a little rundown.

"Is it just you two here?" Julia asked.

"We sometimes have volunteers helping out, but it's just us most of the time," Max said, turning and leaning against the counter. "We're a non-profit organisation. We get a little money from the government, but we stay open mostly from the donations of the kind people in the local community. Sorry, I didn't catch your name."

"Julia," she said with a kind smile. "Julia South."

"It's lovely to meet you, Julia," Stella said, holding her hand out. "If you'd ever want to, we'd love to have you volunteer here."

"I'd love to," Julia said. "I own a café over in Peridale so I could bring over some ingredients and whip something up."

"The people would really love that," Max said as he shook her hand. "I sometimes think they get tired of soup, but it's the only way we can make the most of the ingredients. Most of the stuff we get is what the greengrocers and supermarkets send on when things are ready for throwing away. We toss a lot out because it's already gone bad by the time it gets to us, but we do the best we can with the little we have."

"From what I've heard, the people really appreciate it. I actually wanted to ask you guys a question about the industrial park. You seem to be there quite a lot and I was just wondering if you'd seen anything that might be of use."

"Like what?" Stella asked, her brow furrowing slightly as she glanced at Max.

"Connected to the recent murders," Julia said.

"Murders?" Max looked to his wife, his brows furrowing. "I thought the police said there was no foul play?"

"That's what they think but I have reason to think there's something darker going on."

"That's terrible," Stella whispered as she clutched the cross around her neck. "I'm sorry, but I don't think we can help you. We pull up outside, serve soup and leave. We only see what comes to the window of our food truck."

"I thought as much," Julia said, nodding firmly.

Doughnuts and Deception

"It was worth a shot at least."

"Are you working with the police?" Max asked.

"Not quite. They don't quite believe my theories yet so I'm trying to piece together as much as I can before it happens again."

"We'll pray for you," Stella said, clutching Max's hands. "Be safe, Julia."

Julia assured them that she would, and promised she would be back on Sunday with her ingredients to volunteer. On her way out, she spotted a framed newspaper clipping on the wall from the *Cheltenham Standard*. The headline read '*Local Heroes Help The Homeless*', along with a picture of Stella and Max with a teenage girl standing outside of the soup kitchen. After scanning the first couple of lines of the article, she realised it was their daughter. Glad that there were still good people out there in the world, she smiled to herself and rejoined Barker, Jessie and Tommy.

"How would you like a hot shower and a roof over your head tonight?" Julia asked Tommy as she sat down in between him and Barker. "It's only my old couch, but I'm sure it's comfier than your doorway."

"Bless you, Julia," Tommy said, clutching her hands appreciatively. "You're an angel."

Barker called for a taxi and they all walked outside. When they were on the kerb waiting for the taxi to take them all back to Peridale, Barker leaned in to Julia.

"I thought you could come back to mine to tuck into that trifle you brought," he said. "Finish our date."

"Another time," Julia said. "Jessie needs me right now. I give you permission to eat my portion."

Barker chuckled softly and wrapped his arm around Julia's shoulder. It felt foreign to have a man's arm around her, but she quite liked it. She grabbed Barker's hand and leaned into him. Tonight, she realised how much she appreciated him, and everything else in her life.

When the taxi pulled up, Barker climbed in the front, and Tommy and Jessie climbed into the back. Before getting into the car, Julia looked back at the soup kitchen, but movement in the shadows of the closed nightclub caught her eye. She spotted Pete and Cindy talking to a hooded man. Pete passed over the twenty-pound note Barker had given him, and the man handed over a needle.

Pausing and clinging onto the car door, Julia had to stop herself from going over to slap the needle out of their hands, but she knew she couldn't help them all. Tonight, she was helping Tommy, and that had to be enough.

CHAPTER 8

Freshly showered and shaved, Tommy sat in front of the roaring fire wearing a badly fitting fluffy pink bathrobe. It had been a Christmas present from Sue that Julia hadn't gotten around to forcing herself to wear, so she was glad she could finally find a use for it.

"I feel like a new man," Tommy said as he ran his fingers along his clean jawline. "I underestimated the power of a hot shower."

"You look so much younger," Jessie said as she sat cross-legged on the hearthrug, picking at it with her fingers. "I've never seen you without a beard."

"I don't think I've seen myself without one for years," Tommy said, leaning up and looking in the mirror above the fire again. "Quite handsome, if I do say so myself."

"Your clothes shouldn't be too long," Julia said, as she heard her two-in-one washing machine and tumble dryer click from the washing to the drying function. "Although I must say that colour does rather suit you."

"I think it does too," Tommy said, winking in Jessie's direction. "Imagine what the guys would say if they saw me now. I can't thank you enough for letting me into your home, Julia. You truly are a modern day saint."

"I'm just sorry I can't do more," Julia said, trying to smile despite not feeling very saint-like. "You're welcome to sleep on my couch for as long as you need to."

"No need," Tommy said, shaking his head and waving his hands. "One night will do me just fine. I won't impose. You've done more than enough taking this one in."

Tommy reached out and gently ruffled Jessie's hair. She smiled softly and leaned her cheek on his knee as she stared at Tommy, as though she was looking at a grandfather she adored. Julia recognised that look. It was the look of a girl who longed for a family of her own, and Tommy was as close to that as she had come.

They stayed up chatting until the fire died down and the clock had gone past one in the morning. When Julia noticed Tommy starting to yawn, she suggested they all retire for the night, something Jessie seemed reluctant to do. After Julia dug out her spare duvet from under her bed, Tommy tucked himself up in front of the flickering ambers in the grate of the fire, still snuggled up in the pink bathrobe.

"G'night, little one," he said sleepily to Jessie. "Sweet dreams."

Jessie wandered off to her bedroom, a definite sadness hanging over her. Julia went to her own bedroom and changed into the matching fluffy pink pyjamas for the first time. She looked in the mirror at the hanging sleeves and trailing legs, wondering why her sister thought she would like such things. Chuckling softly to herself, she crept out of her bedroom and along the hall towards Jessie's. Against the soft hum of the tumble dryer, Tommy could be heard softly snoring.

"Jessie?" Julia whispered through the door. "Are you still awake?"

There was a long pause. Julia could tell Jessie was thinking whether or not she should respond.

"Yeah," she replied.

"Can I come in?"

"It's your house."

Julia carefully opened the door, not wanting the creaky old hinges to wake Tommy. She winced as an ear-splitting creak echoed around the cottage.

Sitting cross-legged on top of the covers, Jessie was flicking through a cookbook, looking at the pictures but not reading any of the words. Mowgli looked up from his comfy spot at the bottom of the bed, blinked at Julia, then tucked his face back under his giant tail.

"I found him snuggled up in my laundry basket," Jessie said, reaching out to gently stroke Mowgli's head. "Thought he might be comfier on the bed."

Purring deeply, Mowgli rolled over and arched his back so Jessie could rub his belly. He only did that for people he really liked.

"He's taken quite a shine to you," Julia said,

sitting on the edge of the bed to join in the stroking.

"He's cool. I always wanted a cat."

Julia smiled to herself as she stared down at Mowgli. It was just another thing she hadn't known about Jessie. Just like she had on her date with Barker, she was beginning to realise how little she knew about the people in her life. It wasn't a feeling she liked.

"*Great Cakes of the East,*" Julia read aloud from the front of the cookbook. "Another library book?"

Jessie nodded, the messy bun on the top of her head bouncing. She didn't take her attention away from Mowgli.

"Anything interesting in here?" Julia flicked through the beautifully illustrated pages.

"I don't understand most of the words," Jessie admitted. "Too complicated. I was thinking of trying something to impress you, and then you might want to put it in the café."

"You already impress me, Jessie. You've made a lot of progress with your baking."

"I'm not as good as you though."

"You will be one day," Julia assured her. "A bit more practice and you'll be even better than me."

Jessie smiled appreciatively as she took the cookbook back from Julia. She continued to flick through the pages, pouring over the photographs. It hadn't gone unnoticed by Julia that Jessie had some trouble reading recipes in the café.

"There's something I've been wanting to ask you ever since we first met," Julia started, trying her best to sound casual as she tickled under Mowgli's chin. "Considering everything that's happening right now, I don't think I'll be able to sleep another night without knowing the truth."

"The truth about what?" Jessie asked, looking suspiciously down her nose in a way only she could do.

"About your past."

Jessie immediately looked down and started fiddling with the fraying hem of her pyjama bottoms. She managed to grab a thread with her chomped-down nails and began to pull.

"What's there to know?" Jessie asked, her brows pinching tightly as she carelessly unravelled the stitching.

"Well, I don't really know much." Julia rearranged herself so that she was sitting cross-legged, mirroring Jessie exactly. "All I really know is that your parents died when you were a baby, you grew up in foster care, and then you ran away and I found you in my café."

"Sounds like you already know everything," Jessie mumbled, snapping off the long thread and wrapping it around her index finger.

"They're just facts. You can know a recipe, but it doesn't mean you can bake a cake. I want to know more about Jessie, and how things affected her."

"Nothing's affected me."

"Why don't you start with your childhood?"

Jessie wrapped the thread tightly around the end of her finger and waited until it turned bright red before unravelling it. She exhaled deeply and looked up at Julia, her lips pursed and her eyes narrowed. She looked more uncomfortable than Julia had ever seen her.

"My mum and dad died in a car crash," Jessie said, in matter-of-fact voice. "I was in the car too, but I somehow survived. They say it was because of my car seat and that it was a miracle. Didn't feel much like a miracle to be alive. I was in the system from three months old."

"That must have been tough."

"I was a baby," Jessie said, rolling her eyes. "I don't remember any of it. My first memory was being with this really nice old couple. I thought they were my parents, until they told me they weren't, and that they were retiring from fostering. I didn't understand why they couldn't keep me. It wasn't until later I realised they could, they just didn't want to. I was the last of twenty-seven children they had fostered. I must have been a bad baby."

"I don't think that's true," Julia said softly, resting her hand on Jessie's. "Perhaps they were just too old to look after a little girl. I don't doubt they thought they were doing what was best for you."

"Well it wasn't," Jessie snapped, pulling her hand from Julia's and tossing the thread. "I was four when I went back into care. People only want babies. I bounced from foster home to foster home but everything was only temporary. When I thought I'd found somewhere nice, I'd be turfed back into the care homes. I was always too difficult, or too loud. I never got on with the other kids."

"Is that why you ran away?"

Jessie laughed softly, shaking her head. She looked up at the dark ceiling, and then to the soft lamp on the nightstand, her gaze distant.

"The last family I got put with weren't very nice," Jessie said, still staring blankly at the light bulb. "Kelly and Tim. Along the way, I met some okay foster-parents, but these were the worst of the worst. I don't know how they got approved. It was clear they just did it for the money. Kelly was always at work and Tim was a drunk. There were five kids, two of them were theirs and the others were foster kids. He never hit his own kids. The others just took it, but I was never like that. I told my social worker, but she didn't believe me. She just thought I was being difficult, so I packed my bag, nicked his wallet, and ran."

"That must have been hard."

"Hard?" Jessie scoffed, shaking her head. "That was the easiest decision I'd ever made. The second I left, I was free of being in that messed up system. I slept rough for weeks, and then I met Tommy at the soup kitchen. He took me to Fenton so I wasn't on my own. Took me under his wing like no other foster parent had. There wasn't anything in it for him either. He didn't need to be nice to me. I felt at home there. It wasn't easy, but we got by. It was a long winter, and the older ones were dying all the time, but Tommy looked after me. We'd helped each other, until -,"

"Until what?" Julia urged.

"Until I abandoned him," Jessie cried, her sudden loudness waking Mowgli. "I abandoned all of them because you offered me something better. What kind of person does that make me?"

"A survivor."

Doughnuts and Deception

"But look what's happening to them now," Jessie cried so loud Mowgli jumped up and scurried for the closed door. "They're barely surviving."

"That's not your fault."

"I know," Jessie whispered, dropping her head again. "I feel so guilty because I love the life you've given me. It's the life I always dreamt of but never thought I'd have. You've given me hope, cake lady."

Jessie's words took Julia so much by surprise that she didn't have time to stop the tears gathering in the corners of her eyes. She wiped them away before grabbing both of Jessie's hands.

"You have a home here for as long as you want," Julia said, squeezing tightly. "I promise."

Jessie pulled her hands away and turned back to the lamp, tears collecting in the corners of her own eyes. She furiously wiped them away with her sleeve, her lips curling downwards.

"I've heard that before," she said bitterly. "They say they care, until they have babies of their own, and then they don't care enough to keep you around. You've got Barker."

"We're only dating," Julia said, trying her best to sound reassuring. "No matter what happens, it won't change anything."

"Everything changes," Jessie said bleakly.

"Change can be good. Look at you and me. Before I met you, I was rattling around in this cottage alone. You've given me as much as I've given you. When I wake up in the morning, just seeing you here puts a smile on my face."

"Really?"

"I wouldn't say it if I didn't mean it."

"I know," Jessie said with a nod. "You're an honest woman most of the time."

"Most of the time?"

Jessie smirked a little, wiping the last of her tears away. She looked over to Mowgli as he noisily scratched underneath the door.

"You said you and Barker were just dating, but he's clearly in love with you," Jessie said, meeting Julia's eyes properly since the first time she had sat down. "You don't see the way he looks at you when you're not looking."

Julia smiled nervously, her heart suddenly fluttering in her chest. She tried to deny it, but she didn't know what to say. Jessie was only a teenager, but she was more observant and receptive than people twice her age. She thought about the kiss they had shared earlier in the night before being interrupted by Jessie. She remembered the frustration she had felt when he had pulled away.

Doughnuts and Deception

She had wanted it to last forever.

"I should get to bed," Julia said. "Early start in the morning. Saturdays are always busy."

Jessie nodded and climbed into bed. Julia tucked her in and kissed her on the forehead, and they both smiled at each other. She wasn't the girl's mother, but she knew she had just become the next best thing, and she liked that. Jessie had filled a void in her life she hadn't even realised she had.

"Julia, can I ask you something?" Jessie asked as Julia reached out for the doorknob. "Do you think these people are being murdered?"

Julia looked down at Mowgli, unsure if she should tell Jessie how she really felt. She didn't want to upset the girl, or give her false hope, but in the spirit of being honest with each other, she knew she couldn't lie after everything she had just shared.

"Yes, I do," Julia whispered into the dark. "I'm going to try my best to find out why."

"I know."

Leaving Jessie to go to sleep, Julia carefully opened the creaky door, making a mental note to ask Barker to take a look at the hinges. As she tiptoed back to her bedroom, she realised Barker was filling another void in her life that she didn't realise was empty. It was a void Jerrad had never been able to fill.

Julia crawled into bed and rested her head on her pillow. She closed her eyes, but she knew she wouldn't be able to sleep. Looking up at the dark beams in her ceiling, she decided to make use of her time. Grabbing her laptop, she opened it and started researching injectable poisons that could kill without leaving a trace.

CHAPTER 9

Saturdays in Julia's café were always busy and this one was no exception. While Julia and Jessie ran around the café trying to keep on top of everything, Tommy stood by the sink washing all of the dirty dishes, and doing a good job of it. When Julia promised to pay him for his time, he insisted that the unlimited supply of cakes she had given him throughout the day were more than enough payment. Julia still slipped thirty pounds into his jacket pocket as a thank you.

When the café finally closed, they ate fish and chips before driving Tommy back to Fenton. He turned down Julia's offer of another night on the couch.

Once at Fenton Industrial Park, Julia set up her table once more and served doughnuts and coffee to the grateful inhabitants, some of whom she was starting to recognise. She made a promise to herself that she would keep bringing her coffee and doughnuts as long as the people were there.

"Did you see Cindy anywhere?" Julia asked Tommy while packing up the table and equipment as the sun started to set on Fenton. "I wanted to make sure she was okay after yesterday."

"A lot of people come and go," Tommy said as he shut Julia's car boot. "You get used to people drifting in and out as they please."

Julia hummed her agreement, but Tommy's explanation didn't ease her. After seeing Pete and Cindy hand over cash in exchange for a mysterious needle the night before, she was more than a little worried about the poor woman. When she saw Pete digging around in Mac's corner, she instantly made a beeline for him, leaving Jessie with Tommy in his doorway.

"What are you doing?" Julia asked Pete as he upturned the crates, standing on Mac's broken guitar as he did so.

"What's it to you, lady?" Pete snarled over his shoulder. "I'm looking for money. Mac always had some from his busking."

"The poor man is in a morgue somewhere and you're looking for his money," Julia cried, pushing Pete out of the way to pick up the broken guitar. "Have some respect."

"A man has to eat!"

"I saw you take three doughnuts and eat them all by yourself," Julia said as she tried her best to see if the guitar could be fixed. "I saw you and Cindy last night talking to that man."

"I don't know what you're talking about, lady," Pete mumbled, rolling his eyes and pushing past Julia.

Julia sighed and placed the crates back to how they had been. Sitting in Mac's seat, she looked out at the industrial park with the guitar on her lap. Inhaling the cool night air, she scanned the sea of different faces, noticing how diverse the crowd here was. Some people smiled, some people looked like they were at the end of their tether, and some didn't look like they knew where they were. She wondered if this was why Mac sat here, so he could watch the world pass him by and turn it into beautiful music. Julia ran her fingers along the loose strings. They made a pathetic sound deep within the broken guitar. Cradling it like a baby, she carried it to her car and laid it on the backseat. She didn't know what she was going to do with it, but she knew Mac's legacy deserved better than to be trampled on while people searched for his imaginary pot of gold.

Julia had barely locked her car when a blood curdling cry pierced through the noise, forcing silence to descend on the industrial park. She turned around and saw Pete stumbling out of the burnt out shell of a building, a shaky hand over his mouth. Tommy hurried over, and Pete grabbed his shoulders as he attempted to speak. Sensing what had happened, Julia hurried over.

"She's – She's *dead*," Pete spluttered, clinging onto Tommy as he looked at the ground, looking like he was going to vomit. "Oh my God, she's dead."

"Who's dead?" A woman asked quietly. "Who is it, Pete?"

"Cindy," Julia mumbled under her breath.

"Cindy Gilbert," Pete echoed Julia.

Doughnuts and Deception

Tommy let go of Pete and hobbled into the building, followed by a dozen others. She pushed through the crowd to be by Tommy's side as he lead on. Julia understood what she meant about the man being the leader. Tommy might feel uncomfortable with the title, but people looked to him to take charge.

As they walked towards a burnt out room, which looked as if it had once been an office, their footsteps echoing in the blackened corners, Julia gazed around the shell of the building. Huge chunks of the roof were missing, and it looked as though the rest could fall at any moment.

Tommy pulled back the door with his stick, instantly turning his head away and closing his eyes. Julia stepped around him and looked inside where Cindy was curled up like a baby on a bedding of dirty blankets. There was no way the woman was alive.

Leaving Tommy to shepherd the people out of the building, Julia stood by the door and called for the police, and then for Barker. Before they got there, she crept into the room, wary not to touch anything, but wanting to absorb as much as she could before the unfortunate woman was taken away.

Julia hadn't been there when the other bodies had been found, but she already knew this was different. Cindy's chin was glistening, as though she had been sick before dying. Her arms were littered with small puncture marks, some of them looking fresher than others. A syringe lay next to her body.

When the police arrived, Julia stepped to the side to let them do their job. She wasn't so quick to jump in this time. She joined Jessie and Tommy, who had met up with Barker.

"Has it happened again?" Barker asked quietly, pulling Jessie into Tommy's makeshift home.

"I don't think so," Julia said, careful that they weren't overheard.

"She's as dead as a door nail!" Tommy said.

"I know, but I don't think she was murdered," Julia said with a heavy sigh as she sat next to Jessie. "It's not consistent with the others."

"You're starting to sound like them," Tommy said bitterly, spitting on the ground as he watched the police officers come in and out of the building. "You saw the poor woman, Julia."

"Exactly," Julia said, leaning forward and looking Tommy in the eye. "I saw her in that building, not by the fence where the others were found. She was also a woman. If only three men had died, I might think it was more random, but four shows some kind of pattern. I think they were all killed by some kind of lethal injection, and I think Cindy was killed by injection as well, but by her own hand. I saw a needle next to her body, but no needles were found near any of the other bodies."

"That could mean anything, Julia," Jessie said, shrugging and looking to Tommy for answers.

"I saw something last night," Julia said heavily, looking up to Barker who was still standing, his hands on his hips. "When we were getting into the taxi, I saw Pete and Cindy talking to a man. They handed over money – the money you gave him, Barker – and the man handed back a needle. I think that's what killed her."

"Accidental overdose?" Barker mumbled, almost to himself.

Julia nodded, looking back to Tommy. For a moment, Tommy appeared to not be thinking at all as he stared blankly at the ground. All of a sudden, something seemed to snap in Tommy's brain and he jumped up. Leaving behind his stick, he hobbled across the car park with speed Julia had never seen in the man. He seemed to be searching for someone, and when he found that person, he sped up even more.

"You *killed* her!" Tommy cried, launching himself on Pete and knocking them both to the ground. "You *pig*! You did this!"

"I didn't," Pete yelled as he cowered under his hands. "I didn't mean to. I just left her to sleep it off. I didn't know this would happen."

"This is my fault," Barker whispered to Julia. "I gave him the money."

"It's as much my fault then," Julia whispered back. "I saw it happening and I didn't stop it."

"It's neither of your faults," Jessie said, sandwiching herself between them. "I know these people. They would have found money somehow, Barker. Nothing you could have said would have stopped them getting a fix, Julia. I've seen this happen too many times. I think she had three kids."

"Kids?" Julia asked, her stomach knotting.

"She told me they were taken from her and that's how she ended up on the streets," Jessie said darkly. "She always said she would get clean for them one day, but she wasn't strong enough."

Julia quickly wiped away the tear that escaped, not wanting Jessie to see it. She shook her hair out and ran across towards Tommy. With the help of Barker, they pulled him off Pete. He hadn't actually hurt him; he didn't seem to have it in him. The adrenaline seemed to wear off, and he would have stumbled to the ground without Julia and Barker's support. With their help, he hobbled back to his seat and collapsed, his face dropping heavily into his hands. He started to sob the tears of an exhausted man.

Leaving Jessie to comfort him, Julia and Barker wandered towards the exit. They watched as the paramedics carried Cindy into the back of the ambulance covered by a red blanket. For the second time that week, Julia watched another soul drive away from the only home they knew.

"I've been researching," Julia said, digging into her pocket to pull out the webpage she had printed out in the early hours of the morning. "This is a list of just some of the poisons that can be injected and leave little or no trace."

Barker took the piece of paper from Julia and scanned the list. She could tell he wasn't taking it as seriously as she had hoped.

"This is the stuff of fiction, Julia."

"No it isn't," she said, snatching the paper back. "In fact, most of this can be made so easily with stuff we all have in our cupboards. Potassium chloride, for example. It's one of the things they put in lethal injections for death sentences in America. You can make it by boiling bleach into crystals in your kitchen. It kills instantly and metabolises so quickly, it's practically untraceable. I know they can only test for specific substances if they have a suspicion. If they went in thinking these things were just accidents, they weren't going to look for any of these things. Tell me that wouldn't have happened for any other person."

Barker sighed and pinched between his brows. He didn't disagree because it was obvious he knew he couldn't; he knew she could very possibly be right.

"We still have no proof," Barker said. "I checked. Bailey has been buried, Michael's family claimed him and cremated him, and so did Robert's. There's no evidence."

"And Mac?" Julia asked, pulling Barker out of the way as the police officer walked towards their cars carrying a plastic bag containing the needle. "Have they even started his autopsy yet?"

"I don't have clearance," Barker said firmly, obviously frustrated. "This isn't my case."

"You must know somebody who can help. Somebody you can tell this to."

"They'll think I'm crazy," Barker cried, shaking his head heavily. "I have a reputation."

Doughnuts and Deception

"And what about these people?" Julia cried back, not realising she was even shouting until she heard her voice echo back to her. "You promised you'd help me."

"I didn't promise," Barker said firmly, pointing his finger at Julia.

"I just assumed your word was as good as a promise," Julia said, already turning away from Barker. "I'm sorry I called you."

She walked back to Jessie and Tommy, her frustration and anger growing with each step. Barker didn't deserve to be on the receiving end of that, but she felt desperately useless. She had no idea who could be behind these deaths, and aside from her own theories and research, she didn't have a scrap of evidence. Barker was right. If she took what she thought she knew to the police, she would be laughed out of the station quicker than she could unfold her piece of paper.

Before Julia reached Tommy and Jessie, Tommy jumped up and clutched his stick. He walked right past Julia and headed straight for the gate.

"What are *you* doing here?" Tommy cried, his booming voice silencing the scattered mumblings. "Have you *no* respect? A woman has *just* died!"

Julia turned to see Carl Black, the developer who

had been sniffing around on her first visit to the industrial park. He was accompanied by two men wearing yellow hard hats, and heavy fluorescent jackets, and all three of them stood out in their well-pressed expensive suits.

"You *do* realise *you're* trespassing, don't you?" Carl snapped back smugly, pulling back his sleeve. "As of fifteen minutes ago."

"I've already warned you," Tommy cried, pointing his stick in Carl's face and barely retaining his balance. "Get out of here and leave us alone!"

"I'm afraid I can't do that," Carl said, pushing past Tommy with the two men right behind him. "I'm the new owner of your little hovel, and I'm coming to see what I've bought, and what damage *you* people have done to it."

"Didn't you hear the man?" somebody else cried. "A woman has just died."

"One less of you to clear out," he cried back.

Carl marched forward undeterred, the smug smirk on his face not wavering. The two men behind him looked less sure, half-running, half-walking to keep up with him. She was glad when the policeman standing guard outside of the building wouldn't let Carl pass.

"That man has some cheek," Tommy said as he

joined Julia by her side. "Some people have no humanity left in them."

"Our days here are numbered," a woman said as she walked past. "Where will we go?"

Julia had known this day would come eventually. A piece of land this big in such a great location wasn't going to stay vacant for much longer. She was surprised it had been up for sale for over six months. The fire had cleansed the area, giving it a purpose in housing the homeless, but the developers were about to wipe those people away in the name of progress. It didn't feel very progressive to Julia.

"What now?" Julia asked. "Where will you go?"

"We'll stay here as long as we can," Tommy said. "We're stronger together."

Julia smiled and nodded, but her disagreement was written across her face, and she knew Tommy could see it.

"You don't agree?" he asked, almost offended.

"Maybe it's better to move on?" Julia suggested quietly, watching as Carl and his developer friends walk around the perimeter of the industrial park, pointing things out and scribbling down notes. "You're being targeted here. If you left, the murders might stop."

"And go where?" Tommy snapped, looking

darkly down at Julia. "The world doesn't want us. I wouldn't be surprised if Carl had paid somebody to bump us off to scare us away. It won't work! Do you hear that Carl? It hasn't worked! We're not going anywhere!"

Carl didn't pay him any attention so Tommy cursed under his breath and hobbled back to his spot in the doorway. He collapsed into his blanket and rested his head against the metal door, his thick lids clamping shut. Jessie appeared to be talking to him, but if he was listening, he wasn't responding.

"Are you pleased with yourself?" Julia demanded of Carl as she marched towards him. "Men like you make me sick."

"Men like me, sweetheart?" Carl snickered as he flicked between two pages on a clipboard. "There's nothing dirty about property."

"But there's something dirty about men like you not wanting to help people."

"I donate to charity," Carl said, laughing sourly. "These people don't need my help. They need putting down."

"They're human beings, you *horrid* man!"

"They're a drain on society!" Carl cried, pushing past Julia and continuing with his survey. One of the men smiled an awkward apology at Julia as he hurried past.

She wondered if Carl would think that way if he spent some time here and got to know the people he was judging. Julia had learned so much by being here, and she knew she would never look at the homeless the same again. They were all people with stories and pasts, just like any other person. Carl didn't look at them as being on his level because it seemed easier to disregard their humanity to make it easier to sweep them under the rug.

After collecting Jessie and getting back into her car, they drove silently back to Peridale. She pondered on what Tommy had said about Carl wanting to scare the people away so he could get on with his development. Could money really drive a man to kill in order to get what he wanted? She didn't want to think any person could resort to such drastic measures for something so trivial, but she remembered how he hadn't cared at all that somebody had just died.

"'*One less of you to clear out*'" she whispered Carl's words under her breath as they walked through the dark towards her cottage.

CHAPTER 10

J ulia woke bright and early on Sunday morning so she could volunteer at Stella and Max's soup kitchen. She dressed in the dark, fed Mowgli, and left a note for Jessie under a London Eye magnet on the front of the fridge.

As the sun started to rise in the distance, she drove down the winding lane into the heart of Peridale, slowing as she passed Barker's cottage. The lights were turned off and the curtains were closed. She almost pulled up and knocked on the door, despite the early morning, but she stopped herself. She didn't like how they had left things at the industrial park yesterday, and couldn't help but feel like she would handle the situation better after having had a good night's sleep.

When she was parked between her café and the post office, she let herself in via the backdoor and started to gather up the ingredients she would need to make a lot of chocolate chip cookies. She had decided on it last night after flicking through her mother's old handwritten recipe books because they were easy to make, could be easily replicated, and they always went down a treat. She had yet to meet a person who hadn't fallen in love with her rich, buttery chocolate chip cookies.

Julia poked her head through the beaded curtains and stared at her immaculate café. She loved working there, but she was glad of her one day off a week. If she was honest with herself, she would like another day off during the week so she could relax or go shopping. If she continued to train Jessie the way she was, she might be able to leave her on her own more often without the immense feeling of guilt.

She was about to leave the café when she saw a

shadowy figure running across the village green through the early morning haze. Walking through her café and squinting through the glass, she saw her gran, clutching her skirt as she ran like an athlete. Pulling her keys from her pocket, she unlocked the door as her gran approached.

"Julia!" Dot cried as she breathlessly clutched her sides. "I thought you were a burglar!"

"In my own café?"

"You can never be too careful! Are you opening?"

"I'm just grabbing some things. I'm volunteering at a homeless soup kitchen and I thought I'd make some of my mum's chocolate chip cookies."

"The buttery ones?" Dot narrowed her eyes as she finally caught her breath. "Why do you want to go and do that for? Sounds like a waste of a Sunday if you ask me."

"Because these people need our help and support," Julia said firmly, expecting better of her gran. "What are you doing up so early anyway?"

"It's my turn to stake out the village green," Dot said, glancing over her shoulder at a fold-up chair in her garden. "Me and the girls take it in shifts."

"You're taking this neighbourhood watch very seriously," Julia said through a smile. "You know you're only supposed to keep an eye out, not spy."

"We're not spying, we're staking out. Like in those American cop movies. It's very popular over there, you know."

Julia nodded, wondering where her gran was getting her information. She had expected her neighbourhood watch obsession to have died off by now, but it was taking up most of her time, so much so that she hadn't summoned Julia and Sue to her house for dinner for over a week.

"Found anything interesting yet?"

"Lots," Dot said, barely containing her grin. "Did you know Mary from the hairdressers is cheating on her husband with the butcher?"

"I didn't," Julia mumbled through half-closed lips. "But I do now. Be careful who you tell your information to. You're supposed to be helping the village, not ripping it apart."

"It's all in the name of community spirit," Dot said proudly, crossing her arms under her chest. "Amy Clark is going to take 'round a fruit basket and break the news to Mary's poor husband later today. I don't doubt he's going to be absolutely devastated, but he has a right to know."

"I didn't know you and Amy Clark were friends."

"Well, we're not really. She asked to join and I couldn't say no. What with her being an ex-bank robber and having served hard time – that's what the Americans call prison – I thought she would be a fine addition to our group."

Julia smiled, unsure of what to say. Her gran never failed to surprise her. She wondered if she had been the same way as a young woman, or if her brutal brand of honesty had come with age. If Julia had to guess, she would say her gran was born telling things like they were.

Knowing her gran was only interested in idle village gossip, Julia said her goodbyes and let her gran get back to her fold-up chair and binoculars so she could continue scribbling down the goings-on of the unsuspecting villagers.

After loading up her car, she drove to the soup kitchen, passing Fenton Industrial Park as she did, if only to make sure there wasn't another ambulance taking away another body. She wasn't sure if it was her imagination, but there seemed to be fewer people milling around than yesterday. She remembered what Tommy had said about people coming and going, but she also wondered if the recent string of deaths had succeeded in scaring people away from the now-sold land. Julia knew her theory about Carl killing off the residents of Fenton Industrial Park was a stretch, but it was all she had to work with right now.

"Julia!" Stella beamed from behind the counter as she walked in carrying her boxes of ingredients. "You came! Max, go and give her a hand."

After gratefully handing the heavy boxes over to Max, she joined Stella behind the counter, where she was chopping vegetables for the day's soup. Julia pitched up next to her and started to sift out her flour.

"Baking is a skill I always wished I had," Stella said softly when she had finished chopping the carrots. "God never blessed me in that department."

"You make lovely scones, dear," Max said, diving in to peck her on the cheek. "God blessed you in other ways."

"My scones are like rock cakes," Stella whispered to Julia when Max took the carrots away and dumped them in the giant vat simmering over a low heat. "My husband is too kind."

"Baking is like driving," Julia said as she added in the butter. "Once you learn the basics, you only really start learning for real when you've passed your test. When you have the basic knowledge of why certain things work and how ingredients come together, you'll be able to venture out and start creating your own recipes."

"It all sounds far too complicated for me," Stella said meekly, her fingers brushing over the silver cross around her neck. "I'm more suited to cutting the vegetables. Max has always been the cook."

Julia smiled and nodded. She decided against replying. She wondered if Stella knew she had put herself into an outdated stereotype of what a wife should be. It didn't seem intentional, but it upset Julia all the same. She had been the same way with Jerrad, but it was only when she realised she could fly on her own that she soared. Unlike Jerrad however, Max seemed like a lovely husband. Not wanting to judge how their dynamic worked, Julia turned her attention to sprinkling the chocolate chips into the dough.

"My mother taught me to bake," Julia said when she had achieved the perfect chip to dough ratio. "Without her, I doubt I would be able to make a simple sponge cake."

"Are you close to your mother?"

"I was," Julia said softly, smiling through her pain. "She died when I was a young girl. I still think about her everyday, but I'm not sure if much of what I remember is real, or things my imagination has created over time."

"Your mother is here with you in spirit everyday," Stella said, resting her hand on Julia's, and then immediately pulling it away. "The dead never truly leave us."

It was a theory Julia wanted so desperately to believe in. Over the years, she had felt her mother's presence, usually when she had hit rock bottom. If she felt her mother's presence when she was lying in bed at night, or doing the washing up in her café, she might have believed it was more than her own conscience creating the feelings of closeness. Somewhere in the back of her mind, she held onto the hope that she would see her mother again one day.

"Maybe you're right," Julia said as she chewed the inside of her cheek. "It's a nice idea, isn't it?"

"It's not an idea," Stella said, her pale brows tilting inwards as though it was obvious. "The Bible tells us so. When Jesus died for our sins, he returned to his disciples and walked among them in death. I believe the spirits of our departed loved ones walk alongside us, even if we cannot see them. Those we love never truly leave us."

"Stella, can you take over stirring?" Max called across the kitchen.

Stella smiled meekly at Julia before scurrying off. Julia didn't doubt Stella believed what she was saying. She wanted to believe so desperately too, but her logical brain wouldn't let her believe that her mother was walking alongside her. She glanced awkwardly over her shoulder, wondering if her mother really was there. A cold chill brushed against her neck, making her arm hairs stand on end. It wasn't until she saw Max closing the open back door she realised how silly she was being.

As she started to roll the dough into small balls, she looked over to Stella as she struggled to stir the soup with the giant wooden spoon. Julia wondered what spirit was walking alongside her. The pain hidden under Stella's conviction hadn't gone unnoticed. Reminding herself it wasn't her place to ask, she continued to roll her dough in silence.

By lunchtime, the empty canteen transformed into a hub of activity. Stella and Max's soup went down a treat, as did Julia's cookies. Some of the faces she recognised from Fenton smiled at her, but most of them were different people, only confirming to her how widespread the problem was.

"Do you have a bathroom?" Julia asked Max.

"We don't have a public one, but there's one me and Stella use in the yard."

Doughnuts and Deception

Julia thanked him and pushed on the heavy metal door into the stone yard. The smell of rotten vegetables hit her immediately, radiating from the overflowing uncollected bin in the corner. Clutching her nose she stepped over the rubbish towards the small outhouse. She opened the door and immediately closed it again when she saw Stella.

"I'm so sorry," Julia called through the door, her cheeks flushing from embarrassment. "I should have knocked."

"It's okay," Stella mumbled back as she washed her hands.

Julia thought about what she had seen in the split second she had seen Stella. She had been sitting on the toilet, but she was hitching her blouse up, and she appeared to be injecting something into her stomach. When Stella opened the door, smiling awkwardly down at the ground, she was clutching a small needle with a blue syringe.

"I'm diabetic," Stella said before Julia asked. "Type one. I was diagnosed when I was six, so it's my version of normal."

"I really should have knocked."

"I'm not ashamed of it. It's as normal as brushing my teeth or putting on shoes. God only gives his hardest battles to his strongest soldiers."

With that, Stella hurried around Julia and back into the kitchen. When Julia was finished in the bathroom, she joined her behind the counter as Max started to clear away the bowls and plates from the tables that had already finished and left.

"I didn't think you used actual needles anymore for diabetes?" Julia asked, trying to sound casual. "I could have sworn it was those injectable pen things."

"It is usually," Stella said. "I've been a bit silly. I lost my insulin pen yesterday and I haven't had time to go to the doctors to get a replacement."

"I'd lose my head if it wasn't screwed on."

"It's not the first time either," Stella said as she filled up the sink with hot, soapy water. "I lost it on holiday in the lake district last summer. They didn't have any replacements at the pharmacy. It was a tiny village and there weren't any diabetics, so they gave me some needles and vials of insulin so I could do it the old fashioned way. We ended up cutting our trip short, so when I got back I got my replacement pen. I keep the needles here as an emergency. It's not technically allowed, but God knows I wouldn't abuse them. I would have reported the pen missing sooner, but since Fenton got so full, we've been working all hours God gives us."

"Report it, as in report it to the police?"

Doughnuts and Deception

"There are people out there who abuse the insulin," Stella said, glancing over her shoulder and narrowing her eyes. "Why do you ask?"

"No reason," Julia said with a smile. "I'm just curious."

Stella narrowed her eyes on Julia even further but her expression didn't shift. She busied herself with wiping down the counter, and Julia almost thought her question was going to be ignored.

"So many people are scared of needles, but they have no reason to be," Stella said as she focussed on scrubbing a patch of dried on soup. "The insulin pens are a little cleaner, but I don't mind the old fashioned way. Pain is a part of living."

"I must admit, I'm not the best when I need to have an injection."

"Think about Jesus's pain hanging on the cross," Stella said firmly as she walked over to the sink to wash the cloth. "Even with nails in His hands and feet, He didn't beg for mercy like many expected Him to. He knew He was dying for our sins, and He accepted that He was going to a better place, to join His true father in Heaven."

Julia was beginning to wonder if all of their conversations were going to revolve around stories from the Bible. It reminded her of being forced to sit still in church as a little girl as the priest droned on and on in his monotonous voice about sins and scripture. She had always wondered if she had found the church experience more fun, would her faith be stronger?

"So do you keep a lot on hand for spare?" Julia asked, following Stella over to the sink, where she had already started to wash the large pile of plastic bowls and plates.

"They gave me a two weeks supply that time. It was extraordinary circumstances."

"It sounds like you have a lot left over."

"Why are you so interested?" Stella asked, stopping her scrubbing to turn and look at Julia.

"Oh, my gran was recently diagnosed with diabetes," Julia lied quickly, hoping her cheeks wouldn't burn too brightly. "I just wanted to get to grips with it in case she needed my help."

"She'll have type two. You don't always need to inject insulin with type two," Stella said, returning to the dishes, Julia's lie seeming to wash over her. "Although now that you mention it, there were less needles than I expected this morning."

"Oh?"

"The box seems a little emptier than I remembered," Stella said. "It shouldn't be a problem."

"In the last couple of months?"

"I haven't looked at them for nearly a year because I haven't needed them," Stella said, her tone growing more and more frustrated with Julia's questioning. "Can you pass me that cloth?"

Julia decided she had pushed her luck so she started to gather up her leftover ingredients. As she did, she wondered if Stella's needles had really been misplaced, or if they had been stolen. She knew it was a long shot, but whoever was killing the homeless people could have stolen the needles from Stella's supply, a theory which didn't sit right with Julia. If it were true, it meant a homeless person was killing other homeless people, and that turned Julia's stomach.

When she had packed up her things, she decided she was going to leave Stella and Max to prepare for the evening serving. Stella seemed to be offended by Julia's questioning, so she knew it was better to retreat before the tension grew.

On her way out, she paused at the framed newspaper clipping of Stella, Max and their daughter. As she read through the article, Max joined her and started to read.

"Your daughter is very beautiful," Julia said.

"She was," Max said, sniffing as he adjusted his thick-rimmed glasses. "She died just before Christmas."

"I didn't realise," Julia mumbled, her hand drifting up to her mouth. "I'm so sorry."

"It's okay," Max said, smiling down at Julia to let her know he wasn't upset. "I'd like to say it's getting a little easier everyday, but I'd be lying. I heard you talking to Stella about your mother, so I know you understand the pain."

"Like Stella said, she's here with you."

"If you believe that," Max said, his eyes suddenly glazing over. "Death can send people closer to God in ways one never expected."

With that, he left Julia and joined his wife in the soup kitchen. She finished reading the article before heading for the door. Before she left, she looked back at Stella and Max, who were working silently in the kitchen, not speaking to each other. Their relationship suddenly made more sense to Julia. It was almost as though she could see the strain the death of their daughter had placed on them, but she could also sense how desperately they wanted to cling to each other. It seemed as though dedicating their lives to helping the homeless was a worthy distraction for both of them.

Doughnuts and Deception

After packing her leftover ingredients and equipment in the boot of her car, she drove back to Peridale with a heavy heart and a lot on her mind.

CHAPTER 11

On Monday morning, Julia sat in her café like a customer, sipping peppermint and liquorice tea, and scribbling notes in her pad. She wrote down everything she could think of connected to the deaths, including the list of clues she had gathered, and possible motives. She flipped the page and wrote '*suspects*' at the top in big, bold lettering. After underlining it a couple of times, she realised she didn't have a single one.

"We're running low on cupcake cases," Jessie called from the kitchen. "And icing sugar."

"Hmm," Julia mumbled back as she underlined the word again before flipping to her stock check ingredients list and scribbling down '*cupcake cases*' and '*icing sugar*'. "Anything else?"

"Not that I can think of," Jessie said as she walked through the beads separating the kitchen and the café. "I wrote down a recipe from the cookbook. I didn't know if you wanted to try it or not."

Jessie unfolded a small piece of paper and tossed it to Julia, stepping back and shrugging. Julia read over Jessie's messy handwriting, smiling as she did.

"A Chinese sticky rice cake?"

"I thought it sounded nice," Jessie said, almost apologetically. "It 'sup to you."

"It sounds great. We'll give it a shot this week."

Jessie seemed surprised and smiled awkwardly, looking down at her shoes. Julia scribbled down the ingredients before flipping back to her investigation page. She motioned for Jessie to sit across from her. Julia grabbed two giant cream and jam scones from the display case and set them on the table.

"I've been writing down everything I know

about the case," Julia mumbled through a mouthful of scone as she licked cream from her lips. "It's not a lot."

"Start at the beginning," Jessie said before cramming half of the scone straight into her mouth.

Julia sipped her peppermint and liquorice tea, glancing to the door. The village green was empty, and the few villagers who were out were walking right by Julia's café. She didn't mind. She had come to look forward to her quiet Mondays and was almost disappointed when she was serving more than a couple of customers at a time.

"We have four men, all dead without a real cause of death," Julia started, dusting her icing sugar covered fingers on her dress as she licked the last of the fruity, sweet jam off her lips. "They don't seem to be connected in any way, other than that they are men, homeless and they all died in the same place. We know at least two of them had puncture marks on their arms, but we also have testimonials from people who don't believe they would voluntarily take drugs."

"Bailey wouldn't for certain," Jessie jumped in, mumbling through a full mouth and spitting crumbs as she did. "His folks died from overdoses. He told me when we were back in the system together. He hated it."

"And I spoke to Mac and he told me he didn't touch anything, and that Robert didn't either. Pete also said Father Thind wouldn't, so that's all four men."

"Why haven't the police noticed this?"

"They're not connecting the deaths," Julia said, sighing as she rubbed her brow. "You've got cream on your chin."

Jessie quickly wiped where she was pointing and licked her finger clean. She narrowed her eyes and screwed up her face as though she was thinking hard. When she was finished, she looked sceptically down her nose at Julia.

"Why wouldn't they connect them? It's obvious."

"Maybe, but Barker said they probably don't want to link the deaths because if they do, they're going to be looking for a serial killer. They probably don't want to cause a panic."

"Instead they're just letting them die one by one?"

"It seems that way," Julia said, nodding as she resumed reading her notes. "I've been researching different poisons that can kill people without leaving a trace, and the list seems endless. Most of them can be made quite easily, without many ingredients. It's rather worrying. Most of them wouldn't even show up, even if somebody went looking for them."

"And those needles that were nicked from the soup kitchen."

"That might not be connected," Julia said, tilting her head. "Although it is suspicious. It would certainly give the murderer the means to do what they're doing."

"And it would have to be someone who visited the soup kitchen," Jessie added. "Only homeless people really know about that place."

Julia flicked the page to her list of possible motives. Most of them seemed as far-fetched as the next, but they were all she could think of.

"*Motives*," Julia read aloud. "Somebody is trying to scare the homeless away from Fenton."

"So, the developer?"

"Perhaps," Julia agreed, flipping to the empty suspects page and scribbling down '*Carl Black*'. "That's one suspect."

"One is all you need."

"He certainly seemed cold-hearted enough to do something so evil." Julia circled his name several times. "Money can make people do crazy things. There are other motives though. The other idea I had is that there is somebody with a vendetta against the homeless, so they're taking it out by murdering as many as they can."

"That one wouldn't surprise me," Jessie said, rolling her eyes. "There wasn't a day that went by that I didn't meet somebody who hated me because I was homeless."

"But who?"

"The police?" Jessie offered, drumming her fingers on the table. "Those officers just want to get rid of us to save them the job. They can't rehouse us all."

Julia reluctantly wrote down '*the police*', even if she didn't believe that one. She knew it wasn't impossible, but she couldn't imagine an officer taking the law into their own hands in such a way.

"We also have another homeless person," Julia said, gauging Jessie's reaction carefully. "Perhaps there was a person who was connected to all four of the men, and had a different grievance with each of them."

"What's a grievance?"

"It's like a problem," she said. "A falling out."

Jessie looked down at her drumming fingers and screwed up her face. Julia could practically hear the cogs turning in her brain.

"I don't think so," Jessie said, shaking her head. "They're like a family."

Julia clenched her jaw as she smiled. She believed that Jessie really did believe that because it was all she had had to cling onto for so long, but Julia wasn't so sure anymore. The more time she spent with the people at Fenton, the more she realised they were normal people who didn't always get along, despite their similar situations.

"Besides, who would want to do that?" Jessie asked.

"Pete?" Julia offered. "He doesn't seem to like many people, and he knows how to use needles. He even seems to know people who could supply him with deadly concoctions."

"But murder? That seems a stretch even for him"

"Perhaps," Julia agreed, writing his name down anyway. "There are still so many people I haven't spoken to yet. The murderer could be hiding right under our noses."

Jessie flinched uncomfortably in her seat. It was almost as though they had landed on the same name at the same time, but in very different contexts.

"No!" Jessie cried, before Julia could even say anything. "Tommy wouldn't do that. Why would he?"

"I'm not saying he would," Julia said calmly, leaning forward and dropping her pen. "He's just at the scene every time, and he found Bailey."

"Exactly," Jessie said, forcing a laugh. "Why would he draw attention to a kid he'd just murdered? They didn't always get along, but Tommy wouldn't do that."

"Tommy didn't mention they didn't get along."

"Well, it wasn't that they didn't like each other," Jessie said quickly, stumbling over her words. "Tommy just didn't like the graffiti. He didn't understand it. It was Bailey's way of expressing himself, but Tommy thought he should respect Fenton as their home while they were there. He said if we didn't respect it, people wouldn't respect us. Bailey was a good kid."

"I'm not saying he wasn't," Julia said, reaching out and grabbing Jessie's hand. "You don't have to worry. We're only throwing ideas around. Some of them will sound silly, but it allows us to rule people out. Okay?"

Jessie nodded as she ferociously chewed the inside of her lip. She pulled her hand out of Julia's and fumbled with her fingers in her lap.

"What was Tommy's relationship with the

others?" Julia asked, picking up her pen and hovering over a fresh page. "Just so we can rule him out."

"He liked the priest, even if he thought his preaching was a waste of time," Jessie said as she stared blankly at the empty plate in front of her. "He used to say Michael was wasting his time reading his Bible."

"So they weren't exactly friends?"

"They're not all friends," Jessie said, frowning at Julia. "You can't like everybody."

Julia nodded, not wanting to contradict Jessie's statement that they were all a family who looked out for one another. She had members of her own family that she didn't particularly like, so she knew that didn't immediately make a man guilty.

"What about the banker? Robert?"

"I don't know. They had an argument once, but that doesn't mean anything."

"What did they argue about?"

"Robert fell asleep in Tommy's spot. He was new at Fenton, so he didn't realise not to sleep there. It was only a small thing. They were fine afterwards."

"And Mac?" Julia said, barely looking up as she scribbled all of this down. "What did he think of

Mac?"

"He liked Mac," Jessie said, almost relieved. "Everybody liked Mac, even if his guitar playing kept us awake. Tommy didn't mind, too much. He told him once or twice to stop playing, but it was never anything serious."

Julia wrote down everything Jessie said, almost word for word. She wondered why Tommy hadn't told her these things before. He had acted as though he was friends with all of the victims. The more Jessie spoke, the more it sounded like he had had some kind of disagreement with each victim. As she read back her notes, she knew none of them were enough to drive a man to murder, but months had passed since Jessie had left Fenton, so plenty of murder-inducing arguments could have happened in that time.

Tommy's elderly, kind face appeared in Julia's mind and she immediately felt guilty. The man had been nothing but nice to her, and she was grateful that he had looked out for Jessie in her times of need. The guilt writhed painfully in her stomach as she added his name to her suspects list. She didn't want to believe he could be capable of such terrible things, but she didn't have enough suspects to rule anybody out.

"Tommy didn't do it," Jessie muttered. "He's good."

"I know."

"You know he didn't do it, or you know he is nice?"

Julia's smile wavered. She looked down at the freshly inked name on her suspects list and snapped the pad shut before Jessie could see.

"Both," Julia lied as she gathered the plates and hurried off to the kitchen before Jessie could further question her.

As Julia washed up the two plates as slowly as she could, she mulled over everything. She was so deep in thought, she didn't hear the bell above her café door ring out so she jumped when she turned and saw Barker poking his head through the beads.

"Is it a bad time?" Barker asked as he walked into the kitchen.

"No, you just gave me a fright," Julia said, her hand resting on her chest. "What can I do for you, Barker?"

He was in his usual work suit and camel-coloured trench coat, which told Julia he probably didn't have long. She doubted he was here to take her on another lunchtime picnic, especially after how they had left things on Saturday night. They both tried to speak at the same time, as they stepped closer to one another. Julia laughed and motioned for Barker to speak.

"I'm sorry about the other night," Barker said shyly, pushing back his trench coat and shoving his hands in his trouser pockets. "The stress of this whole thing was just getting to me. I worry about how deep you get into these things, and I reacted badly."

"I can't help it."

"I know," Barker said quickly, looking straight into her eyes. "It's what I love about you. You care about things more than other people do."

Hearing the word '*love*' did something unexpected to Julia's heart. It suddenly started to race, causing her to feel like she was burning up. She attempted to swallow, but her mouth was as dry as an over-baked sponge cake.

"I'm sorry too," Julia said, her tongue feeling like it was swollen. "You're right about caring too much. It's all I can think about right now."

"For what it's worth, I think you're right," Barker said urgently, stepping forward and pulling something from his pocket. "I called in some favours and pushed for them to do a full toxicology report on Mac's body."

He handed the sheet to Julia and the plethora of information boggled her mind. She stared at the list of chemical symbols and combinations she didn't recognise. She shook her head and passed the sheet back to Barker.

"K," Barker whispered, pointing to the top symbol on the sheet.

"I'm a baker, not a scientist, Barker."

"K is the chemical symbol for potassium." Barker folded the paper and stuffed it back in his pocket. "They found a lot of it in his system. More than just a couple of bananas worth."

"Enough to kill a man?"

"That's where it gets complicated," Barker said, taking in a sharp intake of breath through his teeth. "Like you said, some of the lethal poisons metabolise and vanish, barely leaving a trace. This is what it left behind, but alone it's not enough to be ruled as a cause of death."

"But coupled with the needle marks and the others -,"

"There are no others, remember?" Barker interrupted, stepping closer and dropping his voice to a whisper. "The other three were all ruled as inconclusive. They were never looking for lethal poisons, or even a trace of anything. As far as they're concerned, Mac's cause of death is just as inconclusive as the others."

"Surely that's enough to suggest a pattern?"

"Only if they're being linked," Barker said, almost sounding frustrated with Julia. "Aside from their location, these men have nothing in common. They're all completely different ages, with different backgrounds. You're only linking them because you've spoken to people and painted a bigger picture."

"And the police won't because they have no reason to suspect anything?"

"Exactly," Barker said, resting his hand on Julia's shoulder. "You're right about this being discrimination. If this happened in Peridale, the frequency alone would be enough to cause suspicion."

"But because the rate of death among homeless people is higher, this is being looked at as normal."

"Unfortunately that's what's happening," Barker said, deep sadness in his voice. "I was looking into it last night and the statistics made me feel sick. Homeless people are twenty-times more likely to die just because they're homeless."

"Which means the police care twenty-times less," Julia said, pushing her fingers up into her hair.

"This is so frustrating."

"Not all police," Barker reassured her. "We're on the same page now. I'm seeing this through your eyes and it's making me feel awful. I saw homeless people when I lived in the city, but I never cared. Not really. I'd give them money when I could, but I always felt so separate."

"We can help them," Julia said, grabbing both of Barker's hands. "We just have to stop this before it gets any worse."

"How do we do that?" Barker asked, clenching Julia's hands tightly. "Mac's potassium levels aren't high enough to launch an investigation. I mentioned what was happening in passing to the Chief Inspector, just to gauge his reaction."

"I'm guessing it wasn't a favourable one?"

"He laughed and told me to spend my time looking into important things," Barker said, his voice deep with regret. "We're alone."

"When has that ever stopped me, Barker?" Julia said. "We don't need resources to figure this out, we just need to talk to people and keep digging."

"But we don't have a plan," Barker said, letting go of Julia's hands and pushing them back into his pockets. "Or any leads."

"I've got some ideas," Julia said nervously.

Doughnuts and Deception

"You're probably not going to like them though."

CHAPTER 12

J ulia was running down a never-ending corridor
lined with doors. She knew she was dreaming,
but she clutched at the door handles anyway,
sure the answer to what she was looking for was
behind one of them. She ran like she had never ran
in her life, daring to glance over her shoulder as the
corridor melted away in a pool of fire and ash.
Squinting into the dark, she saw a glimmer of light,

beaming through a slit under a door at the far side of the corridor. She knew the answer to what she was looking for was behind that door. She reached out and ran, but she felt like she was walking through mud and her feet were cast in solid cement blocks. Crying out, she was surprised when no noise escaped her throat. She looked back to the door, and it was within reach. She wrapped her fingers around its metal handle. It was different from the others, more ornate and meaningful somehow. She twisted the handle, its surface hot to the touch. She didn't care, she knew when she burst open the door, everything would make sense and she wouldn't have to worry anymore. Icy hands closed around her shoulders, shaking her, dragging her away from the truth. She cried out, but this time she heard her own voice. The corridor and the door melted away and she landed with a thud in her bed, in her small cottage in Peridale.

"Julia," Jessie whispered through the dark, shaking her shoulders. "Julia! Wake up!"

Julia's eyes shot open and she looked up at Jessie. Had she overslept? She blinked into the darkness at the LED display on her alarm clock. It was a little past five, and only four hours since she had fallen asleep researching on her laptop which was still open on the other side of her bed.

"I'm awake," she whispered. "What's wrong? Did you have another nightmare?"

"I wish," Jessie said. "Tommy just called. It's happened again."

"Somebody else has died?"

"Murdered," Jessie said. "For sure this time. It's different."

Julia shook away the last of her sleep and jumped out of bed, climbing into the shape-hugging jeans and baggy jumper that she had tossed across the end of her bed. Before she could even register that she was no longer dreaming and fully awake, she was speeding along the motorway in her tiny Ford Anglia with Jessie in the passenger seat.

When she pulled up outside of Fenton Industrial Park, things immediately felt different. There were more than two police cars, as well as an ambulance, and a forensics van. Julia felt relieved that things were finally being treated differently, but that relief quickly faded when she remembered another man had died.

"Julia," Tommy called over. "Jessie. Over here."

Tommy was standing with a group of around twenty people, as close to the fence as they could get. Officers swarmed around the brightly lit scene, ducking in and out of the white and blue crime scene tape wrapped around the small area. Men in white suits were placing yellow markers on the ground and taking photographs of their findings. In the middle of all of this, a man's contorted body lay, staring lifelessly up at the sky.

"What happened?" Julia asked, shaking the last of the sleep from her mind.

"It woke us all up," a woman said, clutching her heavy coat across her chest. "I heard Jerry scream. There was a man over him, strangling him. Choking him."

"I ran over and I hit him with my stick," Tommy said faintly, barely able to hold himself up. "It was too late. The poor man was dead."

"Strangled?" Julia whispered, shaking her head. "That's not right."

"His arm was all bloody," the elderly woman said. "Like they'd tried to inject him with something, but he put up a fight. That was Jerry till the end. He was a tough old guy."

Julia looked to the scene, squinting through the people coming and going. She wasn't sure if it was her imagination, but she was sure she spotted a needle with a blue syringe next to one of the yellow markers.

"This isn't good," Julia muttered, looking helplessly to Tommy. "This is really bad. Whoever is doing this is getting desperate. They're upping the frequency, and they don't care how they're killing these men now."

"It means they're getting sloppy," Tommy said. "We all saw him."

"What did he look like?" Jessie asked, an obvious shake in her voice as she stared ahead at the scene, seemingly unable to look away.

"Well, it was dark," the woman said, frowning heavily. "And he was wearing a scarf over his face."

"He had a hood too," another woman added.

"But you're sure it was a man?" Julia asked, searching the unsure, shocked faces in the crowd.

"It was dark," the woman repeated.

"It was a man," Tommy said, nodding firmly. "He yelped like a man when I hit him with my stick. I put some force into it too. He almost fell over, but he caught himself, dove through the fence and ran. I called after him, but he was gone before I realised what was happening."

They all stood and watched silently, none of them seeming to know what to say. When forensics had photographed all they needed to, they took Jerry away on a red blanket covered stretcher. They all bowed their heads, apart from Jessie, who still couldn't seem to look away. Julia clutched her hand and they both squeezed, trying to reassure each other.

It wasn't long before the group dispersed and Julia and Jessie settled in Tommy's doorway. Perching on the edge of an upturned plastic crate, Julia shivered, wishing she had remembered to grab a jacket in her tired state. She was more than grateful when Tommy placed a blanket over hers and Jessie's shoulders.

"Where is everyone?" Jessie asked, looking around the bare car park.

"Everyone's moved on," Tommy said through gritted teeth. "Carl Black was here with his megaphone threatening police action. It scared off a lot of them. There were more here when what happened to Jerry woke us up, but that was enough to scare off the rest. We're all that's left now."

"But you've decided to stay?" Julia asked, smiling reassuringly at Tommy.

"It might not be a lot, but this place has become my home. It's all I've got. I'll stay here until the bulldozers move in, and then I'll finally move on. I have no idea where I'll go, but that's no different."

Julia regretted ever writing Tommy's name on

her suspects list. If she had her notepad with her now, she would scratch his name out until she was tearing through to the sheet underneath. In the frustration of trying to place the blame on somebody, she had targeted the wrong person entirely.

"Has Pete gone?" Julia asked, looking around for the drunk.

"He hasn't shown his face since Cindy. He wouldn't dare."

"Did he know Jerry?"

"We all knew Jerry," Tommy said, arching a brow. "He was a big guy. He wasn't difficult to miss. His muscles had muscles. It would take a strong man to wrestle him to the ground and take away his last breath."

Julia mentally scratched Pete's name off her suspect's list. She had seen the drunk, with his shaking hands and wobbly walk. Even if he had managed to somehow strangle a man with his bare hands, she couldn't imagine him fleeing the scene and sprinting off into the darkness.

"At least the police are finally taking it seriously," Tommy said, nodding his head to an officer as they made their way through the small group, asking questions. "Too late for the others though. If they'd have taken this seriously from the beginning, it wouldn't have gotten this far."

Over the next couple of hours, they chatted until the sun rose, the industrial park getting quieter and quieter around them. One by one, the officers packed up and left, as did most of Fenton's residents. When the sun was fully in the sky, there were only a handful of people left, including Julia and Jessie.

"You're welcome to come to my place," Julia offered. "I don't think it's safe here."

"That's what they want," Tommy said, shaking his head. "I don't have many things, Julia, but I have my pride. If they have to take me away from here in a box, so be it."

Tommy pointed his chin to the cloudless sky and squinted into the sun, more defiant than she had ever seen the old man. Julia believed him when he said he would be here until the last minute, she just hoped it wouldn't get to that.

"We need to go," Julia said to Jessie, glancing at her watch. "The café needs opening and we both need to get changed first."

"Go," Tommy said sternly, nodding to the gates. "Don't wait around on my account. I'll be fine. I always am."

Julia and Jessie looked at each other, both seemingly as uncomfortable as the other. Neither of them wanted to tell the man he was being reckless and putting his life in danger for no reason. Despite this, Julia did understand his pride, she just thought it was misplaced. Without the people, Fenton Industrial Park was no more a home than any street corner in any city.

"He'll be okay," Julia whispered to Jessie as they walked towards her car. "He's tough."

"He's being an idiot," Jessie said, looking over her shoulder at Tommy as he curled up into his blankets.

Julia unlocked her car and opened her door. As Jessie climbed inside, she paused, resting her hands on the roof as she looked down the street. Carl Black had just pulled up in a black sports car. He jumped out, a phone crammed between his ear and shoulder. As he swaggered down the street, he clicked his key over his shoulder and the car beeped, its lights flashing.

"Another one's dead," Carl said smugly into his phone as he passed Julia, ignoring her presence entirely. "I'd be surprised if there's anybody left. Call the guys and tell them we'll be able to start demolition in a matter of days."

Doughnuts and Deception

After quickly changing, they drove down to Julia's café, ten minutes late for opening. Dot was already standing outside, tapping her watch as Julia pulled into her parking space.

"Sorry," Julia said as she reached around her gran to unlock the door. "I couldn't get the car started."

Julia glanced to Jessie, making sure that she wasn't going to correct her. Jessie nodded her acknowledgement that it would stay a secret. The last thing she wanted was for her gran and her neighbourhood watch gang wading into things.

"I can't stop," Dot said, pulling up the seat nearest to the counter. "But I'll have a cup of tea, and any cakes if they're going begging."

Julia pulled a slice of yesterday's chocolate cake from the fridge, hoping her gran wouldn't notice it wasn't fresh. She was going to have to spend most of her morning catching up on the baking she had missed.

"Mary's husband didn't take the news very well," Dot mumbled through a mouthful of chocolate cake.

"Huh?"

"Remember how I told you Mary was cheating

on her husband with that lad from the butchers?" Dot mumbled, cramming even more cake into her mouth. "Well, as it turns out, the butcher is gay and actually Mary's cousin."

"So you're telling me your meddling almost ruined a marriage?" Julia said with a sigh as she sat across from her gran.

"How was I supposed to know?" she cried, spitting chocolate cake all over the tablecloth. "They were laughing and joking on the village green like lovers. It's an easy mistake."

"Maybe you should hang up your binoculars."

"Why? Things are finally starting to get interesting," Dot said, wiping her mouth with the back of her hand. "I think the vicar has murdered Amy Clark. She hasn't been to our meetings since last week."

"She's gone to stay with her sister in Brighton," Jessie called from behind the counter. "She told me last week."

"Oh." Dot rummaged in her small handbag and pulled out her notepad, scribbling something down and crossing out something else. "I wonder why she didn't tell me."

"Probably because she knows you don't like her," Jessie called again. "She told me you told her she wasn't a good organ player."

"I didn't say that," Dot protested. "Not exactly. I told her it wouldn't do her any harm to get possessed by the ghost of Gertrude Smith, or at least just her fingers. We all know Gertrude was the better player. The church hasn't been the same since."

"You're unbelievable, Gran," Julia said as she stood up. "And don't pretend you go to church."

"Well, I hear things," Dot said, waving her hands. "Why read the book when you can watch the film? It cuts out all the fuss. I have eyes all over the village. What have you been up to anyway? I feel like I haven't seen you for a while."

"Not a lot," Julia said through almost gritted teeth, glancing back to Jessie who rolled her eyes. "This and that."

"How are things with you and Barker?" Dot asked as she stood up, brushing the crumbs off her pale pink blouse and readjusting the brooch that pinned the collar together under her chin. "Do I need to buy a new hat yet?"

"We're not getting married, if that's what you're saying."

"Chop chop, Julia," Dot said, tapping her watch again. "Time's ticking. You're not getting any younger."

"As you keep reminding me," Julia said, her eyes widening and her jaw gritting. "Me and Jessie will come around for dinner tonight and we can catch up."

"No can do, I'm afraid," Dot cried over her shoulder as she hurried to the door. "I'm holding an emergency neighbourhood watch meeting at my cottage to announce Amy Clark's murder. I'll have to find something else to announce before then, but I've got the whole day ahead of me, haven't I? See you later, girls."

Like a whirlwind tearing through a house, Dot hurried out of the café and across the village green to her cottage, where she immediately took up her post in her garden, peering through her rose bushes with a pair of binoculars.

"Your gran is nuts," Jessie said as she stocked the display case with yesterday's leftovers. "I like it."

Julia spent the rest of the morning baking in the kitchen while Jessie served customers out front. It wasn't like Julia to hide from the public, but she needed time to mull over her thoughts and there was no other time she mulled more than when she was baking. Whether she was cooking up a simple batch of scones, or a more complicated red velvet cake, her fingers did the work while her brain could focus on other things. Baking had saved her a fortune on therapy bills when her marriage broke down.

No matter where she tried to direct her thoughts, she kept circling around to Carl Black. Everything about him and how he acted made her think he was the man Tommy had whacked over Jerry's body. She wondered if a man would be so stupid to show up the same day as the murder, but she knew arrogant men like him didn't think anything they did was ever wrong. Jerrad hadn't seen anything wrong with his affair with his twenty-seven-year-old secretary, nor had he seen anything wrong with packing all of Julia's possessions in black bags and leaving them on the doorstep of their apartment, after changing the locks while she was at work. Men like that didn't have a compassionate bone in their bodies.

"Can I use your laptop?" Jessie asked as Julia flicked through her mother's handwritten recipe book. "The café's empty and everything is cleaned up."

"Sure," Julia said, tossing Jessie the keys to her car. "You know where it is."

Julia landed on the page she had been looking for. She ran her finger over her mother's curly, artistic handwriting. She had always wished her own was more like it, but her fingers were more suited to baking cakes than beautiful calligraphy. She read the recipe for the coconut cake aloud to herself as she gathered the ingredients. She was relieved when she found a packet of desiccated coconut in the back of her pantry.

As she measured out the ingredients, she glanced through the beads to Jessie, who was leaning against the counter and typing slowly on the keyboard. Julia imagined her tongue was poking out of her lips as she focussed carefully on the words. She tried to see what Jessie was doing but she was blocking the screen from view.

After Julia had finished the cake mix, she preheated the oven according to her mother's instructions and poured the sweet smelling mixture into a bundt pan. She always liked how the indented curvature inside of the domed pan made the cakes look. She had no idea if it would look anything like Barker's mother's favourite, but she hoped it would taste just as good, if not better. Her mother's recipe always seemed to elevate the classics, and she had spent many years wondering how her mother had gained her precision and skill when it came to writing out her recipes. Most of Julia's were in her mind, or scribbled down on scraps of paper, which were littered around her café and cottage, some pinned to notice boards, others gathered in boxes in the bottom of her wardrobe.

The timer pinged, tearing her from her thoughts. She had been trying to think of ways to convince Tommy to move on from Fenton Industrial Park. She considered offering him her couch again, perhaps insisting this time. It was a possibility that she would offend him, but she would sleep better at night knowing he wasn't going to be the murderer's next victim.

"Did you know there was another murder?" Jessie asked as she carried the laptop in, staring at the screen.

"Since we left?"

"No, before," Jessie said, placing the laptop on the table. "I just came across this article about a girl who died near the industrial park a couple of months before Bailey died. She was murdered and they arrested the guy."

"I didn't know about that," Julia mumbled, leaning into the screen and scanning over the article. "Does it say how she was killed?"

"Strangled. Sounds like a mugging gone wrong. Those used to happen a lot on those dark paths."

"Is there a picture of her?"

"No, but there's a name. Let me search it online. There might be some pictures on an old social media account."

Jessie copied and pasted the name into the search bar and hit enter. The second the page loaded and the small preview icons appeared, they both leaned back and gasped.

"I know her!" Jessie said.

"So do I," Julia said, quickly dumping the coconut icing over the cake and messily spreading it around the golden surface. "Can you look after the café? I need to speak to Barker."

"Why? What's happened?"

"I'll explain later."

Julia forced the messy cake into a box, ashamed that the icing was practically melting off the still warm cake, but also knowing she didn't have much time to convince Barker of her plan before sunset. She grabbed her jacket and her keys, and jumped into her car, securing the cake in the passenger seat with a seatbelt.

CHAPTER 13

With her cake in hand, Julia knocked loudly on Barker's door, her urgency increasing with each rap of her knuckles on the wood. She pressed her ear up against the door, but she couldn't hear movement, despite Barker's car being parked outside. Inhaling deeply, she knocked until her knuckles hurt. Barker didn't answer, so she tried the door handle. It moved and the door opened. Looking back at Barker's car, she pushed on the wood. It was an emergency, after all.

"Barker?" Julia called out, stepping tentatively down his hallway. "Are you home?"

Splashing water caught her attention so she spun around at the same time the bathroom door opened. Barker stepped forward, soaked from head to toe and covered in bubbles, a small towel fastened around his hips barely protecting his modesty. Julia quickly averted her eyes, but the definition of his surprisingly muscular physique didn't go unnoticed.

"Julia!" Barker cried, dropping his hands to his crotch over the towel. "What are you doing in my cottage?"

"I did knock," she mumbled, turning back to the door. "I'd come back later, but it's quite urgent."

"I was listening to music," Barker said, trying to laugh through the awkwardness. "I like to listen to the radio in the bath on my days off. Helps me forget about work."

"A bubble bath, no less."

"You've got to have bubbles in a bath, Julia," Barker said playfully. "Go through to the living room and I'll throw some clothes on. What's in the tin?"

"Coconut cake," Julia mumbled as she scurried

through to the living room, her eyes firmly planted on the ground. "Just be quick. Like I said, it's quite urgent."

Julia perched on the edge of Barker's squeaky leather couch and waited patiently, her fingers clasped around the edge of the cake tin. The cottage wasn't as clean as it had been on their date, but it was nowhere near as messy as it had been when he first moved to the village. She made a mental note to ask around about a cleaner for him like she had once promised him. He needed a woman's touch around the place, but Julia had enough on her plate than to be cleaning another man's cottage.

Less than a minute later, Barker walked into the living room in a pair of grey sweatpants and a tight fitting white t-shirt, a towel around his neck catching the drips from his damp hair. Now that she had seen his chiselled torso, she could see it through the t-shirt without even meaning to. Had she never noticed before because she was used to seeing Barker in shirts and suits?

"What's so urgent," Barker asked, as he perched on the edge of the couch, his fingers reaching out for the cake tin. "Did you make that for me?"

Julia slapped his hand away, put the cake tin on the cluttered coffee table, and stood up.

"There's no time for cake," Julia said, already heading for the door. "Get your shoes on. I'll explain on the way."

"On the way where?" Barker could barely contain his confused laughter. "I'm not going anywhere looking like this. These are my scruffy clothes."

"Where we're going, it doesn't matter," Julia said, waving her hand over her shoulder as she walked back to the front door. "*Shoes*, Barker! And bring your keys. We're taking your car. Mine is too recognisable."

"You're a piece of work, Julia South," Barker mumbled, and she wasn't entirely sure if she was supposed to hear him.

"I know," she replied regardless.

Five minutes later, they pulled up outside of Peridale's only charity shop, '*Second Loved*'. Whenever Julia de-cluttered her cottage, she would drive down to the charity shop with her unwanted things so Betty Hunter, the sweet owner, could sell them and raise money for various different local charities. She barely took a wage for herself, and whatever profit she made after covering the rent and the bills, she split amongst the most worthy causes in the village.

"What are we doing here?" Barker asked as he peered over his steering wheel at the small backstreet shop. "Have you dragged me away from my bubble bath to dig through a smelly old charity shop?"

"It's not smelly," Julia said as she opened the door. "And yes, that's exactly what I've done. Keep up, Detective Inspector."

Julia hurried into the shop, not turning to see that Barker was following her. She knew he would, if only to find out what she wanted to tell him. Holding back information was something she only did when it felt necessary, and right now it felt more than necessary. If Barker knew the whole plan and her theories up front, he wouldn't go along with it, but if she at least got him halfway through the plan, he might not be so eager to back out.

"Julia," Betty said, peering over her book from behind the small counter in the corner. "What a pleasant surprise. I haven't seen you in a while."

"I don't have any donations today I'm afraid, Betty, but I have come to do some shopping." Julia pushed forward her friendliest smile, not wanting to arouse suspicion before she had even gotten started.

"I got some lovely dresses in last week from a

stylish woman from the city. They'd suit you perfectly and I think they're your size. They're in the back. Let me go and grab them."

"Another time, perhaps," Julia said, just as the door opened and Barker shuffled sheepishly into the shop, looking more than a little uncomfortable. "We're looking for something very specific today. Where do you keep the clothes that nobody ever wants to buy?"

"In that fifty pence bin," Betty said, narrowing her eyes suspiciously over her glasses. "Let me know if you need any help."

Julia assured her that she would. Betty was a sweet lady who lived a simple life. She didn't frequent Julia's café because she thought the prices were too expensive, and she wasn't afraid to let Julia know that. Julia didn't take offence. Betty harked from an era where you could go to the shop with one pound in your back pocket and buy a pint of milk, a loaf of bread, and still leave with change.

"Get digging," Julia ordered, clicking at the basket. "We don't have much time."

Julia started digging in the huge basket of unwanted clothes. Most of what she was saw was garish neon prints that hadn't seen the light of day in over thirty years, but she kept digging regardless.

Doughnuts and Deception

She knew exactly what she was looking for.

"Julia, do I need to call your gran?" Barker whispered. "Have you been sleeping?"

"I'm not having a breakdown," Julia said with a sigh. "I told you I'll explain later."

"Maybe it's delayed concussion? I heard that can happen. It's wasn't that long ago that Terry Lewis hit you on the head with that kettle. Maybe you should just sit down for a second."

"Barker, I told you that I'm fine," Julia snapped under her breath, making sure that Betty couldn't overhear her.

Barker sighed and shrugged, glancing awkwardly to Betty and smiling as she sneered at him. Betty kept to herself, so Julia doubted she had seen, or even heard of the new Detective Inspector in town. She wasn't too fond of outsiders moving into Peridale.

"At least tell me what we're looking for," Barker said as he joined Julia in the digging. "I might as well play along."

"Worn, old, moth-eaten, ruined clothes," Julia said as she pulled a huge, lumpy khaki-green jumper from the mess. "Like this."

"Am I allowed to ask why?"

"It's for a disguise," Julia said carefully as she set

the jumper aside and continued to dig. "We're going undercover and we're going to catch the murderer. I think I know who is behind all of this, but nobody will believe me. I'm not even sure I believe it myself, so we need to catch them in the act."

"Is there anything I can say to talk you out of this insane idea?"

"You know there isn't," Julia said, smiling behind her nerves as adrenaline pumped through her veins. "I'm doing this with or without your help, Barker, so you can either help me and take half of the glory, or you can go home and get back in your bubble bath."

Barker dug in the basket and pulled out a giant, almost destroyed woollen overcoat. He tossed it on top of the jumper and moved next to Julia, nudging her with his shoulder.

"You're going to run into that burning building no matter what I say, so I might as well run in with you."

They silently dug in the unwanted clothesbasket, their hands touching as they weaved in and out of the old garments. Julia tried to think if there was another man in the world who would go along with her without trying to rein her in. Jerrad would have made sure to squash any out-of-the-box thought before it even formed, but Barker let her mind work, regardless of where it took her. In that moment, she was glad she had Barker by her side, willingly and unquestioningly helping her.

CHAPTER 14

J ulia and Barker sat in the car, tucked away in an alley across the street from Fenton Industrial Park waiting for the sun to set. By the time it had faded from the sky and they were surrounded by darkness, Julia had finished explaining her plan to Barker.

"This is mad," Barker grumbled, scratching at the thick scarf around his neck. "Are you sure there is nothing I can do to talk you out of this?"

"I'm sure," Julia said as she tucked her hair into the woolly hat on her head. "We should go. We don't want to miss him."

Julia squeezed herself out of the car and walked out onto the street. She looked down at her heavily layered outfit, hoping she had done enough to blend in, and more importantly, not be recognised. Barker joined her as he continued to scratch at the itchy scarf wrapped around his neck. He yanked his hood up and it fell over his eyes, casting a shadow across the lower half of his face. Julia copied him.

"I wouldn't recognise you," Julia said confidently.

"I wouldn't recognise you either." Barker sighed as he crammed his hands into his pocket. "I'm giving you one last chance to change your mind. What you know might be enough to take to the station and get it investigated."

Julia looked to the industrial park. There were a couple of fires burning, and it seemed that there were more people there than her last visit. She was glad. It would make it easier to go undetected. She wondered if Barker was right. It would certainly be easier to hand over what she had put together, but she also knew she was likely to be laughed out of the station. What she had didn't seem plausible, and yet she knew it had to be the only explanation.

"We should go," Julia said, dropping her head. "Try to act like you belong."

Barker audibly sighed, but he followed her all the same. They walked towards the broken gate, neither of them daring to look up. Julia crammed her hands deep into her pockets, scared that somebody might notice even the smallest detail about her. She knew she was being paranoid, but she didn't want to blow her one chance of ending what was happening.

"Where do we go?" Barker whispered as they walked into the car park and past a group of four crowding around a barrel fire.

"To the fence. That's where the others died."

As they approached the fence, Julia dared to look in Tommy's direction. He was sitting on his doorstep, thumbing through a small book under a heavy blanket. He looked up from his book but he didn't look in her direction. They had gotten away with it, for now.

Two ripped pieces of blue and white crime scene tape still hung from the fence, fluttering in the cool night breeze. Julia brushed her fingers against the cold metal slats, relieved when they budged. She moved down slightly, not wanting to be in the exact same place Jerry had been found only days earlier. Barker pulled up two crates and they sat down across from each other next to the fence.

"What now?" Barker asked as he blew into his hands and rubbed them together.

"We wait."

"What if he doesn't try anything?"

"He will," she said with certainty. "He's getting confident he's never going to get caught. He'll be itching to kill again, if only to prove to himself he can get away with it another time."

"Are you sure you don't want to join the force?" Barker said quietly with a small laugh. "You're better than most of the people at my station."

"I'm sure," Julia said. "I don't do this because I want to, I do it because I have to."

"Part of me thinks you enjoy the thrill."

Julia opened her mouth to disagree with him, but she couldn't. A small part of her knew Barker was right. She would rather not have to keep landing in the middle of murder investigations, but there was something completely addictive about seeing things nobody else did and piecing together the puzzle. Her main purpose was to do what the police wouldn't for the sake of the dead, but she would be lying if she said the adrenaline didn't make her feel more alive than ever.

"These aren't my fights," Julia said, choosing her words carefully. "But I know if I don't do something, this will keep happening."

"I'm not so sure," Barker said as he peeked out of the side of his hood to look around the industrial park. "This is the emptiest I've seen this place."

"Some people aren't so easily scared away," Julia whispered, daring to take another peek at Tommy. "Besides, the murderer is getting desperate. If he can't find anybody here, he'll look in other places. It's not like the country is running out of the homeless. The sooner we get him off the streets, the better."

"I just hope you have this right," Barker mumbled as he leaned against the fence. "Although a part of me hopes you're barking up the wrong tree."

"Me too," Julia said with a heavy sigh. "But I don't think I am."

"After you explained who the dead girl was, I don't either."

Julia joined Barker in leaning against the fence. They both silently stared out at the people in front of them. Julia couldn't believe how different things were from her first visit. The heart and soul of the

Doughnuts and Deception

patchwork community had been torn out, and what had been left behind was sad to witness. The laughter and friendly conversation had been replaced with whispering and paranoid side glances.

"I forgot about Jessie," Julia cried, suddenly sitting up straight. "She'll be wondering where I am. I need to call her."

Julia patted down her jacket, remembering that she had left her phone in her own jacket, which was now locked up in Barker's car boot.

"Does she have her own keys?" Barker asked, patting down his own jacket. "I could run back and get my phone."

"I keep meaning to get her one cut," Julia said, already standing up. "She doesn't even have a phone. Stay here and keep your eyes peeled."

"If she doesn't have a phone, how are you going to call her?"

"Maybe she's still at the café," Julia said, chewing the inside of her cheek. "Or at my gran's. I'm an awful guardian."

"You're far from it. My mum once forgot I was in the back seat of her car and went shopping for three hours. We all make mistakes. Go and call her. I've got things covered here."

Julia smiled her thanks and accepted Barker's car

keys. Walking as quickly as she dared, she headed for the gate, keeping her chin securely pressed against her chest. When she was back out on the street, she ran across the road and towards the alley where they had parked the car. Her heart sank when she saw the dark, empty alley.

"*No!*" She cried with a strained breath. "No, no, no!"

She ran up the street, past the abandoned factories, wondering if she had been looking down the wrong dark alley. She hadn't. Turning on the spot, she pushed her fingers through the heavy hat and clutched handfuls of her curls. She felt completely hopeless. She checked the alley once more, somehow hoping the car had reappeared; it hadn't. Barker's car had been stolen.

Hurrying back, she yanked her hood over her face, her heart pounding in her chest. She looked down the street to the phone box on the corner. She tapped her pockets in vain, but her wallet was in the boot of Barker's now missing car, along with her phone, her cottage and café keys, and her clothes. Once she was back in the car park, her heart sank once more when she saw that Barker wasn't alone.

Suddenly slowing down, she approached Barker and the man who was sitting on her crate, sure that they had been rumbled. When she saw that it was Pete, her heart sank even further. Holding back, she wandered casually into the corner Mac had called home, and perched on a crate, peeping at the men under her hood.

Pete was clutching a can of beer as he leaned into Barker. She tried to focus on what they talking about, but all she could hear was faint, slurred mumbling. She looked over to Tommy, who was looking over to Pete and Barker. She wondered if the night could get any worse.

Julia sat in the corner for what felt like an age. When Pete finally stood up, tossed his empty can to the ground, and stumbled away, she slipped back in and sat next to Barker.

"I thought he'd never leave!" Barker whispered after letting out a long sigh of relief. "I don't even know what he was talking about. Something about aliens and the government. Told me to watch my back."

"Did he recognise you?"

"I don't think so. He didn't say he did. He was three sheets to the wind. Totally wasted. I doubt he even remembers meeting me."

Julia peered under her hood as Pete wandered from person to person, watched tentatively by

Tommy over his book. Those who didn't completely ignore Pete pushed him away disdainfully. It seemed as though he hadn't stopped drinking, or doing a lot worse, since Cindy's death.

"Do you have any money on you?" Julia asked.

"It's in the car," Barker said after patting his pockets. "Did you manage to get in touch with Jessie?"

"No." Julia paused to think about the best way to broach the subject. "About that. Your car is gone."

"*Gone?*" Barker quickly turned to her, frowning heavily. "What do you mean, it's gone?"

"Stolen, I suspect. I'm so sorry, Barker. This is all my fault."

"Are you sure?" Barker said, desperately looking to the gate. "Maybe you were looking in the wrong place?"

"I wish I was. I double checked. It's gone."

"They're going to kill me," Barker cried, dropping his face into his hands. "That was a company car. The boot was full of confidential files that I shouldn't have even taken out of the station. And my phone! And my cottage keys! I don't have spares."

"I think Emily Burns has a spare from when it

used to be Todrick's cottage," Julia offered pathetically. "That's if you haven't changed the locks."

"I haven't," he mumbled through his fingers. "What am I going to do?"

"You can go. There's a phone box at the end of the street. 999 is free to dial."

"I can't dial 999, Julia," Barker snapped. "*I'm* the police. I'm supposed to catch people who steal cars, not let my own get stolen. My boss is going to kill me."

"You can blame it on me. I find honesty is always the best policy."

"Not in this situation," Barker said, fidgeting away from Julia. "I shouldn't even be here. *We* shouldn't even be here. What are we doing?"

"I've already told you that you can go," Julia snapped back, edging away from him and leaning forward onto her knees. "Get a taxi back to Peridale. I'm sure somebody at the station will lend you some money when you get there."

"I'm hardly going to leave you, am I?" Barker whispered, turning to her and half-smiling through his obvious anger. "It's just a car. It's insured. They'll want to know what I was doing in this part of town, but I'll think of something."

"You could tell them it was stolen from outside of the charity shop. We are in disguise after all."

"That's not a bad idea," Barker mumbled under his breath, nodding. "If they have CCTV of us driving, they're hardly going to recognise us dressed like this."

"I was kidding," Julia said, awkwardly laughing.

"I'm not. How are you going to get in touch with Jessie?"

"I don't know," Julia scratched the side of her head as she stared at the ground. "We're in a bit of a mess, aren't we?"

Barker chuckled softly as he looked up. When he looked forward, his eyes quickly widened. Julia followed his eyes to where he was looking, her own eyes widening.

"I don't think you'll have to worry about calling Jessie," Barker said, nodding to Jessie and Dot as they hurried across the car park towards Tommy. "I've always thought your gran was psychic."

"This is bad," Julia muttered, dropping her head. "How did they even get here?"

Julia looked up to see her sister and her husband, Neil, jogging to keep up with Jessie and Dot. Julia dragged her hood over her face and did the same to Barker's. They glanced at each other, half-smirking as they looked down.

"What are they doing?" Julia asked.

"Talking to Tommy."

"They're going to be so worried about me."

"Just go and talk to them."

"I can't!" Julia glanced up and watched as Tommy stumbled to his feet with Jessie's help. "This will have all been for nothing if we blow our cover."

"Like you said, they'll be worried."

"I'll explain it all later," Julia said, shrugging and biting into her lip. "They'll understand, won't they?"

"Who are you kidding?" Barker asked, glancing up and dropping his head immediately. "I've met your gran. She'll be furious you didn't ask her to join our undercover operation. I doubt she'll ever speak to you again."

Julia laughed as quietly as she could, leaning into Barker's shoulder. Taking her by surprise, he picked up her hand and looped his fingers around hers. She almost pulled back, scared it would blow their cover, until she decided it didn't matter. She told herself it would look more convincing if they were holding hands, even though she just enjoyed the feeling of his thumb stroking the back of her hand.

"I've got an idea," Julia mumbled, pulling away from Barker and standing up. "Stay here and try not to make any more friends."

"Where are you going?"

"I'll be back in a couple of minutes," Julia whispered over her shoulder. "Don't worry. I'll fix this."

Julia ran along the edge of the fence, pulled back the loose slats, and slipped through the gap with ease. Once on the other side, she paused in her tracks, staring out into the dark winding path ahead, her eyes playing tricks on her. The shadows shifted and danced, the impossible blackness bringing forward her childhood fear of the dark. Just like the monster under her bed, she knew it was her imagination taunting her. Monsters didn't hide in the shadows never to be seen, they walked among the living, and she knew the monster she was searching for wouldn't come out until he was sure he wasn't going to be caught.

Julia walked around the edge of the industrial park and lingered by the broken gate. Staring ahead at the road, she didn't dare move or lift her head until she heard her gran's loud and distinctive voice.

"She's *dead*!" Dot cried. "I just *know* it! I have a *fifth* sense, you know."

"It's a *sixth* sense, gran," Sue replied. "And I've already told you, knowing Julia she's probably off somewhere getting herself into trouble, thinking she's doing the world a favour."

"Well if she's not dead yet, she *will* be by sunrise!" Dot snapped back. "You mark my words, young lady. Your sister is up to no good. She can't just keep her nose out of other people's business."

"Bit rich, coming from you," Sue mumbled back.

Julia looked up from her hood as the voices moved closer. She watched as Sue and Neil walked back towards her car, followed by Dot and Jessie. As loudly as she dared, she coughed deep within her throat, hoping it was enough to catch Jessie's attention. It wasn't. Watching them walk back to the car, she looked around desperately, landing on an empty beer can. Wrinkling her nose, she picked up the can, closed one eye and threw it at Jessie. She clasped her hand over her mouth when it bounced off Jessie's head.

Clutching her hair, Jessie spun around, ready for a fight. Julia waved her over, her finger pressed hard against her lips. Jessie glanced over her shoulder at the others, before running quickly towards Julia.

"What the *hell* are you doing?" Jessie cried as Julia yanked her into the shadows. "Have you completely lost the plot? What are you wearing?"

"It's a long story," Julia said, pulling back her hood a little and grabbing Jessie's shoulders, looking over to the car. "I need you to tell them I called you and that I'm out for dinner with Barker, but you have to wait until you're back in Peridale."

"You're hardly dressed for dinner," Jessie snapped, looking down her nose. "You stink, you do know that, right?"

"I know. It's stuff I grabbed from the charity shop."

"You look homeless."

"That's the point, Jessie," Julia said, sighing and rolling her eyes. "Just do what I say? Please? I'll explain it all tomorrow."

"Tomorrow?" Jessie's eyes suddenly widening as she seemed to figure out what was happening. "You're trying to catch him, aren't you?"

"No."

"You're lying," Jessie muttered through tight lips. "I can always tell when you're lying. Your cheeks always go red. It's the same look you give me whenever you try one of my cakes."

"It's not," Julia lied again. "Please, just go back to the car and do what I asked."

Julia looked over Jessie's shoulder to the car, but like Barker's, it was nowhere to be seen. In the distance, she saw Neil's car drive around the roundabout and take the turning back to Peridale.

"Looks like you're stuck with me," Jessie whispered smugly. "Your gran is so busy planning your funeral she didn't even notice I wasn't there."

"They'll come back looking for you," Julia said desperately, her cheeks burning hotter than ever. "Just go and wait over there."

"They won't find me when they get here." Jessie pulled her hair back and fastened it in the small of her neck with the hair tie she always had wrapped around her wrist. When she was done, she pulled her black hood down to her eyes and zipped the front up to her chin. "You're not the only person who can go in disguise."

"You can't be here," Julia whispered, looking up and down the street for a sign of a way out. "He's not going to approach if he sees you."

"You told me you didn't know if I was a boy or girl when we first met." Jessie hunched her shoulders, looked down and crammed her hands in her baggy jeans' pockets. "Remember? I can handle myself, Julia."

Julia saw more of herself in Jessie than she liked to admit in that moment. She wondered if this was what Barker felt like every time Julia refused to back down from one of her ideas. Knowing there was nothing she could say to her young lodger to change her mind, Julia reluctantly turned on her heels and walked back around to the narrow path leading back to the gap in the fence.

"There's somebody there," Jessie whispered, putting her arm in front of Julia. "Up ahead."

"My eyes did the same thing to me."

"No, seriously." Jessie yanked Julia into the trees and dragged her down behind a bush. "You need to get your eyes tested, old lady."

"Less of the old."

Julia peered over the bush, quickly darting down again when she saw the figure Jessie had seen. Wearing a dark trench coat, he pressed his nose up against the fence, only metres away from Barker.

"Let's get him," Jessie whispered, ready to spring up at any moment. "You hold him down, and I'll sock him on the nose."

Julia had to practically wrestle Jessie to the ground to stop her from springing up and launching herself at the man. Resting her hand over Jessie's mouth, Julia peered over the bush once more, and watched as the man disappeared back the way he came.

"Get off me," Jessie said as she yanked Julia's

hand away. "You just let him get away."

"It might not have even been him."

"Who even is *he,* anyway?" Jessie asked, standing up and brushing the leaves and dirt from her jeans. "How am I supposed to know who to attack if you don't tell me?"

"You're not going to attack anyone, do you hear me?" Julia said, wincing as Jessie helped her up from the ground, the creak in her knees reminding her she was more than double Jessie's age. "You're going to sit quietly, and not ask too many questions, okay?"

"Sure," Jessie scoffed. "You're funny when you want to be."

They walked back to the fence and Julia held out the slats for Jessie to climb through. Keeping her head low and her hands in her pockets, she walked along to Barker and sat down. As Julia pushed herself through the gap, she looked around to make sure they hadn't been seen, and it didn't seem like they had.

"This was your plan?" Barker snapped as he pulled Jessie in. "Are you crazy, Julia?"

"I have ears," Jessie replied, leaning into Barker and scowling. "I'm not a kid. I'm seventeen next month."

"You're a kid in the eyes of the law."

"The law can kiss my -,"

"I didn't have a choice," Julia jumped in, apologising with her eyes to Barker. "They drove off without her. They'll probably come back to look for her when they realise."

"Too bad I'm staying here," Jessie said, rubbing her hands in front of her mouth. "It's just like old times. Shall we start a fire?"

"I have a terrible feeling about this," Barker said, sighing and shaking his head. "I'm going to wake up in my bubble bath and this will all have been a bad dream."

"You have bubble baths?" Jessie mocked, snickering under her breath. "Who's the little girl now?"

Julia stopped herself from laughing, instead smiling under her hood at Barker. Exhaling and frowning, he leaned against the fence, crossed his arms and closed his eyes. The people were showing no signs of going to sleep anytime soon. It was going to be a long night.

CHAPTER 15

Julia's eyes shot open. She knew she had been asleep for more than a couple of seconds. Blinking into the darkness, she pulled her coat tighter around her body. It hadn't been so cold when she had closed her eyes. Sitting up straight, she let out a long yawn, noticing how eerily quiet things were. The fires had died down and everybody had bedded down for the night. Barker's snoring next to her told her she wasn't the only one who had allowed herself to rest her eyes.

When her pupils adjusted to the blackness, she looked ahead and noticed a slim figure moving away from her in the darkness. Remembering Jessie, Julia jumped up.

"Jessie," Julia whispered into the dark. "Where are you going?"

"I saw something near the gate," she whispered back over her shoulder. "Don't worry, I've been keeping watch since you fell asleep."

Guilt surged through Julia as she fast-walked to catch up with Jessie. How long had she been asleep? Just from the temperature, it already felt like the early hours of the morning.

"What did you see?"

"I thought I saw a man walking past."

"Thought?"

"It's dark," Jessie whispered before letting out a long yawn. "It's been a long night."

Julia's guilt increased. How could she have put them all at danger by being so stupid? She glanced back at Barker as he slept peacefully by the fence. Why did she have to drag other people into her mess? She wished she had done it alone, with a flask of strong, hot coffee.

Doughnuts and Deception

They reached the street and the warm safety of the streetlights. The road was completely silent in either direction, the only movement coming from the soft shadows of clouds rolling past the pale yellow, almost-full moon.

"There's nobody here," Julia whispered, moving in closer to Jessie. "Let's get back to Barker."

"I saw a man," Jessie said, ignoring Julia and walking down the street. "It could be *him.*"

"It was probably just a trick of the light," Julia whispered, jogging to keep up with Jessie. "Let's just get back to Barker."

Jessie suddenly ground to a halt, putting her arm out to stop Julia. She turned around, her expression angry and firm. Julia's heart sank. She knew what was coming next.

"You left Barker, a man, alone next to the fence where men are being murdered?"

Julia's heart sank to the pit of her stomach. She didn't realise she was running until she felt the wind rip back her hood, tear off her hat, and unleash her curls. Almost in a daze, she could feel Jessie directly behind her as she rounded the corner back into the industrial park.

When Julia saw a shadowy figure climbing through the fence, her heart sank even further, but when she saw a second figure climbing through, her heart practically stopped. She wanted to scream out for Barker, but her vocal cords were paralysed.

"There's two of them?" Jessie cried, hot on Julia's heels.

"I – I didn't know," Julia said, unsure if her words were vocal or just in her mind. "I didn't know."

When the bigger of the dark figures grabbed Barker, Julia let out an ear-piercing screech, but she didn't hear it. Her legs ran faster than they had in her life, outrunning the girl half her age. Barker's eyes shot open, but before he could scream out, the figure's hand wrapped around his mouth. The second, smaller figure pulled a needle out of their pocket, their hands obviously shaking.

"Do it!" the bigger figure, a man, cried. "Do it *now!*"

"*Stella!*" Julia cried, grinding to a halt metres from the fence, her palms darting up in front of her. "Drop the needle, Stella!"

Julia's use of the smaller figure's name had been a guess, but when the woman turned and looked at Julia, fear alive in the whites of her eyes through the balaclava, Julia knew her guess had been correct.

"I have to do this," Stella mumbled, her hands

shaking so out of control it looked like she had just been dunked in a cold bath. "It's God's will."

"Is this woman for real?" Jessie cried.

Julia edged closer, her hands outstretched and her face kind. The man yanked back his balaclava. Julia wasn't surprised to see Max.

"Stella, don't listen to her," Max growled, his teeth bared like a dog ready to attack. "You know God spoke to me. Spoke to *us*!"

Stella nodded, fumbling with the plastic end of the needle. She yanked it off and dropped it to the ground, some of the poisonous solution falling from the metal tip. Julia saw it drip to the ground as though in slow motion.

"God spoke to us," Stella said, echoing her husband. "He wants us to make the world a better place."

"By murdering innocent people?"

"God was vengeful, Julia." Stella turned to Julia and pulled back her balaclava, a deranged, sweet smile consuming her pale, slender face. "When God spoke to Noah and told him to build the ark, he told him to save the animals, not the people. The people needed to be taught a lesson. They *needed* to die."

"What is this woman on?" Jessie cried. "Somebody call the police!"

Barker started to scream behind the gloved hand, his eyes wide and staring at Julia. She felt as though she was looking into the eyes of a dead man. She held back her tears, knowing she had to remain strong. She had to fix her mess.

"I know what happened to your daughter," Julia said, taking another baby step forward. "Bethany. I know she was murdered by a homeless man, right there on that path. I know she was walking him back from the soup kitchen, and that he attacked her. I can't imagine what that feels like, but this isn't the answer."

"You're right," Max spat, his nose so wrinkled and tight, he no longer resembled a human. "You can't know what that feels like. None of you can. We did nothing but *help* these disgusting people, and that's how they repay us? By taking our daughter?"

The crack in Max's voice broke Julia's heart. For a moment, she saw the eyes of a grieving father, not a murderer.

"Just because the awful, evil man who took your Bethany was homeless, it doesn't mean you need to punish every homeless person."

"We're making the world a better place," Stella repeated. "They're a disease."

Doughnuts and Deception

"I know you don't believe that," Julia whispered, stepping closer, her palms spread wide. "You put your love into your soup to help these people. You care about these people."

"God -," Stella started, her voice trailing off as her bottom lip wobbled uncontrollably.

"God wouldn't ask you to kill," Julia said, smiling through her own pain. "Would he, Stella? Remember what you told me about the dead? They never really leave us. What would Bethany say if she saw you like this? You said she walks beside you. If that's true, she's here right now, seeing you do this."

Stella looked desperately from Julia to Max, searching for answers from the devil and angel on her shoulders. Max tightened his grip on Barker, his arm secure around his throat. Beads of sweat trickled down Barker's bright red face, his eyes darting from Julia to the shocked crowd that she could feel gathering behind her.

"Max?" Stella pleaded. "What does God say?"

"I think Max lost his faith when you lost Bethany," Julia whispered, stepping within reaching distance of the needle. "Isn't that right, Max? You can't speak to God any more than I can."

"I'm tired of this," Max cried, his grip tightening so firm around Barker's neck that the Detective

Inspector's eyes started to flutter. "Give me the needle, Stella."

Out of the corner of her eye, Julia spotted movement. She didn't turn to look but she could sense a slow, lumbering figure edging closer to Max. She wanted to cry out, to stop them doing anything stupid, but she couldn't take her eyes away from Barker's fluttering lids.

"Stella," Julia choked, unable to hold back the tears anyway. "You loved your daughter, didn't you?"

"Of course she did!" Max barked. "We both did!"

"Well, I love this man," Julia stepped forward, not caring if Stella lashed out with the needle. "Don't take him from me before I've even had a chance to get to know his middle name, or his favourite colour. Please, Stella. I'm not a mother, but you know I understand loss. Remember when I told you about my mother? I understand your anger. I *understand* your desperation to believe you're doing the right thing, but you're not. This is your first time even holding a needle at somebody, isn't it? All the other times Max was on his own, wasn't he?"

Stella nodded, tears streaming down her face as she stared down at the needle.

Doughnuts and Deception

"I didn't understand when he told me what he had done, but when he told me it was an order from God, I knew we had to finish his mission."

"There's no mission," Julia mumbled through her tears. "Please stop this."

The lumbering movement came into Julia's full view, and she involuntarily turned her head. So did Max, but not quick enough to duck out of the way of the solid gas canister heading for his skull. With a solid thud, Max let go of Barker, swayed on the spot for a moment, and collapsed into a groaning heap.

"Enough talking," Tommy cried, dropping the gas canister and stumbling into the fence, his legs giving out without the aid of his stick. "Hold him down, boys."

Three men rushed forward, all of them jumping on Max like a pack of starving dogs on a sliver of meat. She expected them to hit the unconscious man. She wouldn't stop them if they did. To her surprise, they just pinned him to the ground.

"I'm sorry," Stella whispered, her eyes as wide as the moon in the sky as she lifted the needle up. "Bethany, Mummy is coming."

Julia heard her own cries echo around the industrial park. She dove forwards, her hand clutching Stella's wrist. The frail woman didn't fight. She relaxed her hand and dropped the needle to the ground. In that moment, every muscle in Stella's body seemed to vanish and she crumbled like her husband had. Julia caught her, and they both fell to the ground. As Stella sobbed, Julia wrapped her arms around the poor woman's shoulders and pulled her in, as though she was her mother. She felt every ounce of her grief, every drop of her pain, every tear she had shed for her daughter. That agony consumed Julia. She didn't try to hold back her own sobs.

Through her tears, she opened her eyes to see Barker clutching onto the fence, gasping for air. She knew some of her tears were for him. Her declaration of love echoed around in her mind and she sobbed even harder, the fresh tears from a place of relief and elation, rather than pain.

Police sirens echoed in the distance, letting her know it was all over. She released her grip on Stella and let Jessie help her up off the ground.

"I thought she was going to kill you," Jessie whispered through her tears as she buried her face into Julia's heavy overcoat. "You're so stupid."

"I know," Julia said, gripping Jessie's head tight to her chest. "I'm so sorry."

As uniformed officers stormed the scene, Julia

Doughnuts and Deception

caught Barker's eyes. Through his pain, he smiled at her. Rubbing his neck, he staggered forward, wrapping his arm around the both of them. He pressed his lips against Julia's head, his palm gripping the back of her head so tightly she couldn't help but feel safe. None of them let go until officers pried them apart, demanding statements from all of them.

CHAPTER 16

Julia had never been in her café at sunrise, but as she hugged a mug of peppermint and liquorice tea behind the counter, she began to wonder why she wasn't there every morning to witness the vibrant orange sky illuminating the grass.

"*Julia!*" Dot cried as she stormed through the cafe full of everybody who had been at Fenton when Max and Stella had been arrested. "Oh, Julia! I thought you were dead!"

Julia set her mug on the counter and let her gran hug her tightly, until she practically couldn't breathe. When she finally managed to pull her away, guilt flooded her when it became obvious her gran hadn't slept.

"What on *Earth* is going on?" Dot cried. "Who are all these people? Where's Jessie?"

"I'm here," Jessie stood up from the table she had been sharing with Tommy, pulling her hood down. "Come with me, I'll explain everything."

Jessie looped her arm through Dot's and practically dragged her through to the kitchen as she stared around the full café, her mouth opening and closing, the questions appearing to flood her brain faster than her mouth could process them. Julia mouthed her thanks to Jessie, who winked in return.

"I've said it before, and I'll say it again, you're an extraordinary woman, Julia," Tommy said, motioning to the seat across from him. "Not many would do what you did tonight."

"I'm a stupid woman," she said as she sat down, glad to be off her feet. "I almost got Barker killed."

"If you hadn't been there, it would have been one of us."

There was a chorus of mumbled agreement

through the mouthful of free cake and coffee.

"I'm just glad it's all over," Julia said, letting out a sigh of relief.

"When I said not many would do what you did, I wasn't just talking about trying to catch that evil man," Tommy said thoughtfully as he leaned back in his chair. "A lesser person would have let Stella Moon take her own life."

"It wasn't even a decision," Julia said over the second chorus of mumbled agreement. "She's already been through enough."

"And that's what makes you so great," Tommy said. "You did them all proud. Bailey, Michael, Robert, Mac, Jerry – you did those men proud tonight."

A round of applause ran through the café, and Julia smiled as gratefully as she could, even if she didn't feel very worthy of the applause.

"How did you figure it out?" A woman asked through a mouthful of Victoria sponge cake.

"I didn't really," Julia said with a sigh, her eyebrows drifting up her forehead. "I owe that to Jessie. She was looking online, trying to find some help for you guys, *you* especially, Tommy. She did a search for Fenton, and she came across the article about Bethany Moon's murder just before

Christmas."

"That was all a terrible business," Tommy said regretfully, bowing his head. "She was a lovely girl. Frank Benton was a monster. He wasn't one of us. He might have been homeless, but he wasn't welcome at Fenton. We all knew what he was capable of. There were rumours. I wish I could have done something to protect that poor girl. Maybe none of this would have happened if I was firmer on him."

"This isn't your fault, Tommy," a man said, leaning over and slapping him on the shoulder. "You've always tried your best for us. You were right there till the end."

It suddenly struck Julia that none of them could really go back to Fenton Industrial Park, tonight, or ever. Now that Carl Black owned it, it wouldn't be long before work started on his luxury apartments, and a new community of people moved in. Julia scrambled her brain for a way she could help, but like Tommy had already told her, she couldn't help them all.

"Frank Benton took that poor girl's life, and they didn't even throw the book at him," Tommy said, his voice dropping to barely above a whisper. "I was there in court the day they sentenced him. They gave him life, but life doesn't mean life anymore, does it? He could be out in fifteen years with good behaviour."

"That man doesn't know how to behave," another man jumped in. "He stole my only pair of shoes, y'know."

"Took my jacket," somebody else added.

"He took a girl's life," Tommy reminded them. "I'm not surprised her father was driven to the brink of insanity."

"Using God as an excuse!" The man jumped in again. "That's the real crime here."

"Max Moon lost his faith," Julia said, looking up at the ceiling, wondering if she had gained some in her experience tonight. "He killed those men not in the name of God, but in cold-blooded revenge. I suppose he killed Bailey to try and fix the pain, and when it didn't work, he kept doing it."

"And what about the wife? She was in on it too."

"I believe her when she said she didn't know," Julia said firmly, shifting in her seat. "I volunteered at their soup kitchen not long ago, and I know she didn't know then. I'm certain of it. She's diabetic, and she told me a box of her needles had gone missing. I knew it was connected, I just didn't expect that it was her husband who had taken them."

"What did they even inject?"

"Potassium Chloride," Julia said. "Or at least that's what I think. High levels of potassium were found in Mac's body. We'll never know with the others, but I'm confident it was the same throughout. Of course, he strangled Jerry to death with his bare hands because Jerry wasn't such an easy target."

"How could a man like that even know how to get something so lethal?" Tommy whispered, leaning across the table.

"It's all out there on the internet," Julia said. "One quick search and you've got a recipe for murder. All you really need to do is boil down some household bleach and you're already halfway there. I wouldn't be surprised if he was cooking it up in the soup kitchen in the dead of night while Stella slept."

"Frank Benton was a monster, but Max is just as bad," Tommy said, stamping his finger on the table. "Grief isn't an excuse for murdering five men!"

"I agree," Julia said with a nod. "But it does explain it, at least. There's never an excuse for murder."

"I wouldn't mind getting my hand's around Max's throat!" The same man jumped in. "An eye for an eye, I say."

Julia's café door opened, and Barker walked in, dark bruises on his throat. She immediately jumped up, leaving the conversation before it turned nasty. She hurried over to Barker, desperate to know what his examination had discovered.

"Light bruising and swelling," he croaked, rubbing at his purple throat. "It will heal itself, but I will be talking like I've got a frog in my throat for the next couple of weeks."

"That's perfectly fine with me," Julia whispered as she pulled him into a hug. "You're okay. That's the main thing. Did you manage to find out what's happening to Max and Stella?"

"They've been taken to Hesters Way station in Cheltenham for questioning. It's out of our hands now," Barker said as he pulled away from the hug. "I do have some good news though. They found my car abandoned on a country lane, all smashed up, but they recovered what was in the boot."

"Small victories," Julia whispered with a wink. "Sit down, I'll make you a nice hot cup of honey and lemon tea for your throat."

Barker sat across from Tommy, and Tommy immediately shook Barker's hand. Julia peered through the beads and chuckled when she saw her gran gasping in horror as Jessie explained everything that had happened, her hands telling most of the story. When she wrapped her hands around Dot's throat, Julia knew she was probably embellishing a little. She didn't doubt Jessie's version of events would be around the village by midday. Julia wouldn't be around to find out. For the first time since opening her café, she was putting a '*CLOSED*' sign in the window, and her and Jessie were going to catch up on some much needed sleep, if their minds would allow.

"I'm disbanding my neighbourhood watch!" Dot exclaimed as they thrust through the beads. "I'm clearly not up to it!"

"This didn't even happen in the village," Julia reassured her jokingly. "I'm not sure your binoculars would stretch all the way to Fenton."

"Even so, I should have spotted the signs that you were up to something," Dot said regretfully before kissing Julia on the cheek. "I better go and call Sue to let her know you're okay. She'll be worried sick sitting by the phone."

"Apologise from me, okay?" Julia asked. "Tell her I'll call her later."

Dot nodded and waved her hand as she walked through the café, eyeing the heavily dressed men and women with suspicion as she went.

One by one, the last remaining residents of Fenton Industrial Park went their separate ways, some of them leaving together, some leaving alone, but all of them making sure to thank Julia before they went on their way. She wanted to ask each of them where they planned to go, but she stopped herself, knowing she wouldn't like the answers. There was one person she could help today though, and she wasn't going to take no for an answer.

"Tommy, you're coming to mine," Julia ordered as she grabbed her jacket. "After a nice long sleep, and a relaxing bath, we're going to figure something out for you."

Tommy stood up, laughing and shaking his head as he rested his weight on his stick. He walked over to the door, and Julia almost thought he was going to leave, but he opened the door and waited for them. With Barker and Jessie by her side, they walked out into the fresh morning air. She looked up at the pale sky, more grateful than ever for breathing the fresh air of a new day.

"Are you going to join us, Barker?" Julia asked as they walked towards his cottage.

"I think I'll resume my bubble bath," Barker said as he unhooked his gate. "I suspect I'll have to run a fresh one, but I'd like to finish my soak and pretend all of this never happened. Well, maybe most of it at least."

He winked at her before turning and heading towards his cottage. She knew exactly what part he was talking about, and it caused a smile to spread across her face.

"You so love him," Jessie whispered, jabbing her in the ribs as they walked up to their cottage. "I told you he had the hots for you."

Smiling up at the sky, Julia didn't even bother denying it. She had meant it when she said she loved Barker. She didn't know how or why, she just knew she did, and it had never felt so good to admit it to herself, possibly for the first real time in her whole life.

CHAPTER 17

When Julia returned from the shops late in the afternoon, Jessie was still fast asleep in bed. Julia's own sleep had been cut short when Mowgli had pawed at her face, so she had decided to make use of the day after a prolonged soaked in the bath with a cup of peppermint and liquorice tea.

"Afternoon," Tommy said as Julia dumped the

shopping bags on the counter. "I hope you don't mind, but I used your house phone."

"Not at all," Julia said as she shrugged her coat off, walking through to the hallway to hang it on the hat stand by the door.

"She's been out like a light all morning," Tommy said with a gentle smile. "You can almost pretend she's a normal kid when she's asleep. I didn't sleep much myself. How can you after what happened?"

"Who did you call?"

"I decided to swallow my pride and call my brother," Tommy said, his fingers nervously drumming on the countertop. "I haven't spoken to him in fifteen years, but he still had the same number. It's the only one I know by memory. We talked a lot of things out, and I'm sure we're going to talk even more over a couple beers, but he said I can go and stay with him and his family up in Manchester until I get back on my feet."

"That's amazing news."

"Seeing you and Jessie together reminded me what family meant," Tommy smiled tightly as he glanced up at the ceiling. "I've been hiding from mine for too long. It's time I faced my mistakes and got my life sorted out. I have you to thank for all of this, and before you tell me it's what anyone else would have done, it's not. Not at all, Julia South. They don't make them like you anymore."

Julia didn't argue. Tommy's words touched her, so all she could do was smile her thanks before filling the kettle to make him a coffee. As long as he was her guest, she would continue to look after him.

"I'll cover your train fare," Julia said as she poured fresh milk into the coffee. "I won't take no for an answer."

"I hadn't even thought about that," Tommy chuckled. "I suppose I'll have to join the rest of the world and start worrying about money. I'll pay you back when I'm sorted out. My brother thinks he can get me a cleaning job at the place he works at. Part time, but I'm not far off retirement as it is."

"I won't accept a penny from you," Julia said as she set the coffee in front of him. "Have you eaten?"

"You're going to make somebody a great mum one day," Tommy said with a soft smile. "Well, I suppose you already have actually."

At that moment, Jessie staggered through from her bedroom, her long, dark hair matted at the side and her eyes still half-closed.

"What time is it?" She croaked.

"Just gone four."

Doughnuts and Deception

"I slept like a log," Jessie muttered through a yawn.

"Us too," Tommy said, sending a wink in Julia's direction.

Jessie climbed onto a stool next to Tommy, her hands instantly diving in for his coffee. He let her take it, so Julia refilled the kettle and made him a second cup.

"I got you a present in town," Julia said as she fished through the bags. "I know it's not your birthday until next month, but this is separate."

Julia placed the mobile phone box, which had been gift wrapped in red paper with a white bow, in front of Jessie. She rubbed her eyes, and frowned up at Julia, staring down her nose in the way only Jessie did.

"What is it?"

"Open it and find out," Julia whispered, leaning against the counter. "It's a token of my appreciation for you staying awake all night and keeping watch over us."

Jessie forced out a yawn as she ripped back the packaging. Her eyes widened when she saw the shiny, white mobile phone box.

"The man said it was the latest model," Julia said, unsure of what Jessie's reaction was. "He said all the kids have this one."

Jessie looked up at Julia, and then down to the box, and then to Tommy. Julia wasn't sure if the stunned silence was a good one, or a bad one.

"I've never had my own phone before," Jessie mumbled as she opened the box.

On top of the phone was the metal key Julia had had cut from the spare she kept under the plant pot next to the front door.

"I thought it was about time you had your own key," Julia said, her voice shaking with nerves. "Since this is your home now too."

Jessie picked up the key and clenched it in her fist. She looked up at Julia, and it become obvious she was holding back tears. They smiled at each other, and Julia let her know it was okay not to thank her verbally with a little wink.

"You'll be able to call me on that gadget," Tommy said, pointing to the phone in the box. "I'm moving up to Manchester to stay with my brother for a little while."

"Your brother?" Jessie dropped the key onto the counter and turned to Tommy. "Manchester? You can't!"

"I can, and I am," Tommy said, resting his hand on Jessie's shoulder. "You've coped without me all of these months, and rightly so. Julia is your family now, and you couldn't ask for a better mother."

Julia rested her hand on her chest, determined not to let another tear leave her eyes today. She had cried enough over the past twelve hours to last her a lifetime.

"I'll miss you," Jessie whispered, dropping her hair over her face.

"I'm only a train ride away," Tommy replied, tucking her hair behind her ear. "When I've got my own little place and I'm all settled, you can come and visit me. Promise?"

Jessie nodded, but she didn't look up. Julia could tell she was silently crying under her hair. As tough as Jessie wanted to act in front of other people, when it came to her family, she was still a vulnerable girl, and they were both the only family she had. Julia made a mental note to hold Tommy to that promise. She didn't doubt for a second that he wouldn't try his best to keep it.

After they finished their coffees, there was a knock at the door. Julia left Jessie and Tommy chatting in the kitchen and she hopped over Mowgli and into the hallway. Through the frosted glass panel, she made out the outline of Barker. Smiling like an excited schoolgirl, she pulled open the door.

"Afternoon, madam," Barker said, both of his hands behind his back. "I have a special delivery for a Julia South."

Barker pulled a bunch of two-dozen white roses from behind his back, and peered over the top, his eyes glittering at Julia.

"Who are they from?" she asked playfully, a grin spreading from ear to ear as she accepted the bouquet.

"A very charming and handsome man," Barker said as he stepped into the cottage. "But he wasn't available to deliver them, so you're stuck with me instead. I have something else for you too."

Barker pulled a plastic bag from behind his back and Julia let out a huge sigh of relief when she saw her clothes, her purse, her phone, and her keys. She had been embarrassed asking Sue to drive her to the shops, and to pay for everything, but she was relieved to know she could pay her straight back.

Julia took the flowers through to the kitchen and put them in a vase of water. Jessie and Tommy both smirked, glancing knowingly at each other. Barker hung back and tossed the bag onto the couch as Mowgli circled his feet.

"Can we go somewhere and talk?" Barker asked.

"*'Talk'*," Jessie mocked under her breath.

Doughnuts and Deception

Julia pursed her lips at her, before turning to Barker and noticing the sudden seriousness of his expression. She put the flowers on the counter, blocking Jessie's face, and walked through to her bedroom, motioning for Barker to follow.

"Is this about Max and Stella?" Julia asked quietly as she closed her bedroom door. "Sit down."

Barker perched on the edge of her bed, exhaled heavily and looked up at the low-hanging beams in the ceiling, the seriousness of the bruises on his throat all the more obvious.

"Sort of," he said as she sat next to him, glad she had made her bed that morning. "Max is singing like a canary, telling them everything. He's still going with the God line, but they know it's a load of codswallop. Stella only really knows Max's version of things, so I think they're leaning towards her being more of an accessory, or at least attempted murder, but that depends on the judge she gets. We all heard and saw her, and the main thing is, she stopped, so I think a jury will look favourably on her. Max, on the other hand, he'll never breathe the air as a free man again. I'll make sure of that."

"I hope somebody takes over the soup kitchen," Julia whispered, staring at the rug against her dark floorboards. "It would be a shame if the good they did do stopped now."

"I love that your mind goes straight there," Barker said softly, nudging her gently with his shoulder. "I'm sure somebody will."

"At least it's all over."

"Yeah," Barker mumbled uncertainly.

"You don't sound so sure?"

"There was something else."

"What?" Julia edged forward and turned to him, her brows pinching together as she attempted to read the dark expression taking over his face. "What's happened?"

"This isn't your fault," Barker said, grabbing both of her hands tightly in his. "I want you to know that."

"What's not my fault?" Julia said, trying to sound firm, but her voice shaking.

Barker inhaled deeply, glanced up to the ceiling, and then down to her, a forced smile pushing the corners of his lips up.

"I'm under investigation at work," Barker said, dropping his head to the floor. "For operating outside of the official borders and for putting civilians in danger. I couldn't deny any of it after my statement and my involvement."

"Investigation?" Julia replied, shaking her head.

"What does that mean?"

"It means they're going to look into my conduct," Barker said, his voice darkening. "They're going to try and see how well I do my job, and if I deserve to keep it. I've been suspended without pay until they make a decision."

Julia pulled her hands away from Barker's and jumped up. She immediately started to pace her bedroom, her hands disappearing up through her hair. How could she have been so blinded by her own need to discover the truth? Had it been worth destroying Barker's career?

"Are they going to fire you?"

"Not necessarily." Barker jumped up and grabbed Julia's shoulders, forcing her still. "You did the right thing. *We* did the right thing. You were right about them never believing you. After Jerry, they had been questioning Carl Black and they were close to charging him because he didn't have an alibi. He might not be a very nice man, but he's not being charged for a murder he didn't commit because of you."

"But this has ruined your life." Julia sighed heavily, leaning into Barker's hand as he rested his palm on her cheek.

"Far from it," Barker whispered, pulling her in

closer. "Even the darkest clouds have silver linings. You said a lot of things when you were trying to get Stella not to kill me. I wouldn't blame you if you stretched the truth to get through to her."

"I meant every word," Julia said automatically without taking a second to think about it; she didn't need to.

Barker pulled her in and he softly brushed his lips up against hers. All of the stress, and the trouble her meddling had caused melted away. She was old enough to know happy endings didn't exist, but she felt as close to happy as a person could be in that moment, and that was enough for her. They pulled away, their eyes slowly opening and their smiles spreading.

"I love you too," Barker said, cupping both of her cheeks in his hands. "And since you asked, my favourite colour is green, like your eyes, and my middle name is Fergus. Don't ask. My mother was Irish."

"But you love your job too," Julia mumbled, her stomach knotting out of control as her heart thumped wildly in her chest.

"It's just a job," Barker said, shrugging and letting go of Julia's face. "Some things are more important."

Doughnuts and Deception

Hand in hand, they walked through to the kitchen. Julia didn't care about Jessie's sideways glances, or even what the village would say. They could talk all they wanted because she had realised what, and who was most important to her. Tommy had been right about family being important, but she knew he hadn't just been talking about the family people are born with, but the family people choose. The people at Fenton Industrial Park had been a family, Jessie and Tommy were family, and Julia felt like she had just added three new people to hers.

Inhaling the floral scent of the white roses, she squeezed Barker's hand and smiled at Jessie through the petals as she hugged Mowgli, knowing she was more than ready for whatever life threw at them next.

If you enjoyed *Doughnuts and Deception*, why not sign up to Agatha Frost's **free** newsletter at **AgathaFrost.com** to hear about brand new releases!

Coming April 2017! Julia and friends are back
for another Peridale Café Mystery case in
Chocolate Cake and Chaos!

Made in the USA
Middletown, DE
29 March 2017